Radha

By

Shakuntala Rajagopal

To Dear Ray & Lily Sasthy

Best wishes

lots of memories

Love, Shakuntala Rajagopal

This book is a work of fiction. Any resemblance to actual events or persons, living or dead, is entirely coincidental.

"Radha," by Shakuntala Rajagopal. ISBN 978-1-60264-093-1.

Published 2007 by Virtualbookworm.com Publishing Inc., P.O. Box 9949, College Station, TX 77842, US. ©2007, Shakuntala Rajagopal. All rights reserved. No part of this publication may be reproduced, stored in a retrieval system, or transmitted in any form or by any means, electronic, mechanical, recording or otherwise, without the prior written permission of Shakuntala Rajagopal.

Manufactured in the United States of America.

Cover design by Peg Miller
Cover painting of *Kovalam Beach* by Shakuntala Rajagopal

Dedication

To:

Sarada Ammachi, my maternal aunt, who instilled in me a love of books, and who disciplined my keen sense of expression by demanding a synopsis of a page, a chapter, or a book once a week in my formative years.

Acknowledgements

I would like to express my gratitude to my friends at the Barrington Writer's Workshop for years of ongoing support, for patiently listening to my revisions, for their constructive analysis each time, and in helping my story move forward without losing my voice.

Thanks to Lisa Guidarini for final edits and friendly support, and to Peg Miller for incorporating my artwork in the cover design.

If not for Helen Gallagher, I would still be revisiting and revising my story instead of releasing it for all to enjoy. Thank you.

A big Thank you to my family, Devi, Molly, Nimmi, Suresh, Don, Niko and Travis for their understanding of my need to tell this love story that has filled my thoughts and my dreams for years, and for encouraging and supporting me to see it in print.

And above all my deep appreciation to my dear husband Balu Chettan, for giving me the space and time to live out Radha's life, her thoughts and her dreams, and patiently enduring my frustration at times when foiled plots and Radha's tears needed my focus and attention late at night.

Chapter One

Kovalam Beach
1965
Give me the glowing sun, the waving coconut palms,
And the fragrance of white jasmines... and you give
me paradise.
        Shakuntala Rajagopal

The day that Radha first met Danny was marked indelibly in her mind. It was at Kovalam beach, an unspoiled gem of a tropical ocean paradise, ten miles away from Trivandrum, that he first entered her life.

Mid term examinations in Anatomy were over and a handful of "medicos", as the medical students were called, from Trivandrum Medical College, had gathered at Kovalam beach for a weekend break before the next rigorous sessions of Anatomy - Physiology - Biochemistry started.

Anyone who went to Kovalam beach was forewarned of the fickle nature of the ocean in this part of the world. The private bus taking the noisy young crowd had taken an unusual route. As they went up winding hills and precarious curves Kamala shouted from the back of the bus, "are you sure this is the way to Kovalam, we are not going to Sabari mala (Sabari hills), we are going to the beach." The bus echoed with laughter.

Turning a curve, miles of velvety green paddy fields bordered by statuesque coconut palms offered a breathtaking vision of God's country. Before anyone could comment on what they felt, a deep glazy emerald ocean replaced the expanses of paddy fields. The unexpected, precipitous transition quieted even the most vocal among them. The bus fell silent.

Kamala grasped Radha's hand. "Oh my God, Radha."

Radha replied in a hushed voice. "Even though I have come here before, this sight takes me by surprise every time."

Kamala nodded.

They were best of friends. No one would suspect that two people so different could be such good friends. Radha was a willowy, gracious young lady. She moved slowly, was never the first to board a bus, and always waited to be spoken to before she said anything, except to those close to her. Kamala was petite, always in motion, and had an opinion to say about everything that went on around her. There was never a dull moment when Kamala was around. Radha often looked out for her, like laying a hand on her arm to stop her from irritating the surgery professor, who did not want to be interrupted during his lectures.

Kamala moved to the front of the bus to get a better view of the approach to the ocean and the special beach.

One of those unfathomable reactions that a human being experiences rarely in her lifetime, Radha muttered to herself, waxing poetic as her favorite poet Rabindranath Tagore would.

Kovalam beach is so unlike any other beach that I have known, Radha mused. As they came closer to the sea, and eventually traveled downhill to reach the seashore, more surprises awaited. White sands appeared between the deep emerald green of the sea and the mossy green paddy fields. Blue-green waves splashed into white foam as the waters spread themselves thin over the sands again and again. More treats were in store, just half a mile away. The rocks. Dark massive rocks rose suddenly out of the sea and came upon them as if in a horror movie. Radha could never anticipate how the ocean would behave from hour to hour, even though she had visited this beach on many previous occasions. No words could express or even start to explain the changes in the patterns of the waves and the sea. One minute it would be lying there calm and inviting, and then, without warning, a monster within would wake up with a roar and the waves would start pounding the beaches and batter the rocks in a violent frenzy that brought fear even in the bravest of hearts.

As they alighted from the bus and walked on to the hot sand, Radha turned to Kamala. "It always makes me feel that the two faces of the Goddess Devi are revealed side by side, in this part of the ocean."

"What do you mean?" Kamala was curious.

"On one side the benevolent Goddess Lekshmi, goddess of peace and prosperity, and on the other, the Goddess Durga, the fierce one..."

"You are right Radha, the angry waves remind you how Devi Durga achieves her missions to save the world in a fashion of vengeful violence," Kamala completed the explanation.

The two friends understood each other very well.

A volleyball landed between the two girls, followed by Renu and Veena who came barging to retrieve it. Now, any chance of a decent conversation was history.

"Come on, Kamala, the guys are waiting. The net is up and it is our chance to beat them at volleyball today."

Renu tugged at Kamala's arm, and Veena had a grasp on
Radha's arm. Radha firmly, yet gently freed herself from
Veena, and shook her head. She was in no mood for any
strenuous activity.

Kamala laughed. "All right. I am coming."

The three girls left Radha alone and joined the
others at the beach, where a net waved as though it was
welcoming them to release the tension and energy that had
built up for the exams they had just taken.

Radha breathed a sigh of relief in escaping their
clutch, and picking up her book of poetry by Tagore,
walked away from the rambunctious crowd, and the noise
on the beach.

She walked towards The Kovalam Palace, a majestic
mansion that was once a beach retreat for royal families.
Following the Indian Independence, the various kingdoms
were taken away from the Kings in an effort to unify the
newly freed India, and to establish a sense of equality in
the populace. The Kerala Government converted this beach
palace into a rest house for dignitaries who needed
overnight accommodations. The Palace was graced on all
sides by lush, green, fruit bearing trees and surrounded by
wavy coconut palms or kerams, after which Kerala, the
land of the coconuts, is named. Palm groves stretched all
the way down to the water, even over much of the rocky
slopes.

Radha went around the building to the rear of the
palace, to a verandah, high above the sea level, and away
from the sandy cove on the beach where the volleyball
game was in progress. To her relief, this area was well
protected from the noise of her comrades' rowdy revelry.
Yet, she could see the vast ocean and hear the waves.
Radha sat down on the wide stone steps facing the water
and opened Tagore's *Gitanjali*, her constant companion-
book.

Radha felt eyes upon her, and turning around she saw him as he came around the large pillared entrance to the rear of the palace. A guitar was swung over his left shoulder, and his wild, wavy hair was held back in a rubber band. His beard, scraggly as it seemed, was trimmed purposely to give an air of abandon. They had never been introduced; but she had no trouble recognizing the famous rebel in the group, the one and only "*Danny Boy.*"

Daniel Mathew was known for his unconventional ways, not only to all his co-medicos, but also to the collegiate students in the neighboring colleges of Arts and Sciences, Engineering, and Law. He was the ultimate Hippie. In the sixties, even among the jean-wearing anti-establishment students in town, he stood out as the one that was untamable. Known to question all rules, he was a thorn in the side of all the professors. Yet they knew him to be a bright, honest, and sometimes even gentle, young man. He was a true enigma that neither the professors nor his classmates could understand.

Oh no. He is coming my way. Radha watched him approach. *I wonder why people say Danny is a troublemaker? I realize many of the professors do not like his flagrant denouncements of the bureaucracy in evaluating the exams. But the last time I saw him with his patients, I felt that they really loved him. I know they look forward to his rounds, when he gently eases their pain with appropriate care. I also remember how he made the really sick old man laugh, with his not so subtle joke about the pretty girl that was just passing by.*

"I am Danny," he said without any affectation in his voice. "Who is this angelic vision in front of me? Did you just rise from the ocean? How did I miss you on the bus?"

Radha was silent. She was not one who talked much anyway, and the unexpected compliment left her tongue-tied.

"But," he continued, "I am glad to get away from the crowd and also from my own guitar and songs. I hope you won't mind if I just sit here by you?"

It was more of a statement than a question and it really did not matter what she wished, because without waiting for an answer, he put down his guitar and sat a step below hers. He seemed not to be concerned with who she was.

Radha felt uncomfortable in his presence, but could not tell him so without sounding rude. She kept her silence.

Her dark curly hair fell in wavy cascades around her face and reached almost to the ground as she sat on the steps. The side-strands were pulled back in a shiny black clasp towards the back, but the clasp was there in vain and in no way able to handle the unruly curly locks which had escaped from its control and fluttered around her lovely face in the sea wind. She kept brushing them back in an endearingly self-conscious motion with her long fingers, fingers that looked as though they should belong to an artist. She wished she could get up and move away from him, yet she could not understand why she did not.

After what seemed to be a long while, Danny turned his face up to her and extended his right hand, as he spoke, "I'm sorry to intrude...and your name is...no, don't tell me." He paused. "I want to call you *Maya*, illusion, for truly you must be magical, because it is too good to be real that a lovely maiden such as you would sit here alone, waiting for me. I hope you don't mind my calling you Maya." He jabbered on, not giving her a chance to answer. Hesitantly she took his hand in a handshake. Her mind and heart were in a jumble, as if in the throes of a wild wave. She could not figure out why she felt so discombobulated by the gesture. He was just another medico. Why was she in such a state?

She found her voice at last and spoke. "My name is Radha - Radha Menon," she laughed lightly, easing the tension in the air. "I am not really a 'Maya'. But, oh..." She had just realized that he still held her hand in his, and abruptly pulled it back.

He looked innocent and vulnerable, seated on those steps there and gazing up at her. The slanting rays of the evening sun made his brown eyes even lighter than they seemed at first, and there was an expression in them that she had never perceived in any other pair, an expression that tugged at the deepest core of her heart. She did not know what to make of such feelings.

Thus they sat gazing at each other as if in the same dream that both were dreaming, until the silence was broken by "Radha, where are you?" Renu and Kamala came around the corner of the palace calling Radha's name.

"We were wondering where you were." They stopped and fumbled as they realized she was not alone.

"We thought you may have gone into the ocean by yourself, and we were really worried."

Radha took her eyes off Danny's face slowly, reluctantly, and made the proper introductions. She could not remember exactly what she said.

As if a perfect stone sculpture came to life, he stood up and gaily addressed the two friends...the magic was broken...the world was a noisy place once more.

Radha did not bother to say goodbye, as she left him at the steps of the Kovalam palace, and returned to the cove where the remaining medicos were, with Kamala and Renu.

The volleyball game was over, but the argument as to who had the best shot was still going on. In another corner, the umpire, who was their Anatomy Demonstrator, himself a young doctor who had completed the medical curriculum barely two years prior, was vehemently defending his call on a play contested by the losing team.

The strong smell of curried rice and meat puffs laid out on folding tables under the shade of the coconut palms proved too inviting to continue the arguments. As they centered on the food, they thanked Naani Amma profusely for leaving her kitchen at the women's hostel to bring them their special favorites. Naani Amma was more than a cook there; she was their special friend.

Beach blankets were spread over the sand and they sat in small groups talking and eating, while an occasional couple walked along the water's edge, young lovers too full of blooming romances, to be hungry for real food.

From the corner of her eye, Radha noticed Danny making more trips than the rest for refills of his plate, which to her appeared already full. Her cheeks turned red, considering the possibility he might be looking for an opportunity to talk to her. She was starting to worry that Kamala might also notice Danny's extra trips to the food table, when someone shouted, "Look at that sky."

Time had flown so quickly. It was almost sunset. The horizon was aglow in shades of gold and yellow with streaks of orange, and the clouds mirrored the pattern of the waves beneath, both lit up by the setting sun.

Radha stood up, hugging her book, and walked towards the water, facing the sun, allowing herself to be filled with the harmony and balance that a setting sun brings.

She was startled by a whisper, "What does Tagore have to say about such a glorious sunset?" Radha dropped her book on the sand. Turning around she saw Danny was close by her side.

He leaned down, picked up her book and dusted the sand off, before handing it back to her. She hoped he did not notice how her hands trembled as she took the book from him. Then, without a word, he was gone.

For the rest of the weekend Radha did not run across Danny, and she was relieved. But she did not quite understand why she felt such relief. On the way back to the college, she saw him enter the bus and sit down two seats ahead of her. A sudden yearning that he would come back and talk to her was quickly replaced by panic in her mind that he might do so. She felt split in two. Why was she so intrigued by him? The confusion lingered within her, even as she returned to her room at the hostel.

Chapter Two

*Do not keep to yourself the secret of your heart, my
friend!
Say it to me, only to me, in secret
You who smile so gently, softly whisper,
my heart will hear it, not my ears*
        Rabindranath Tagore

Upon their return to Trivandrum Medical College
Radha immersed herself in her rough schedule. Mornings
started out with seven a.m. sessions in Anatomy
dissections. She was part of a foursome that was dissecting
a left leg. Following the course of the Femoral artery from
its origin from the Iliac, and defining what branch fed what
part of the leg, had held great fascination for Radha in the
past; but this particular week she kept losing track of the
course of the major arteries, and could not remember the
names of their branches.

"What is wrong with you, penné, girl?" Kamala, her
dissection partner, kept needling her for a reason for her
distraction. "Would you please come back to earth so we
can complete this dissection before the mean Professor
Pandyan appears and throws us out of this room?"

Radha made efforts to concentrate on the task at
hand, but to no avail.

After a whole morning of futile nagging, Kamala said in desperation, "Radha, you look drawn and wan and I think you are coming down with the flu. I would greatly appreciate if you would not lean so close over our field of dissection, so you don't give the rest of us whatever it is that you are suffering from." Often they crowded curiously close to the field of dissection in order not to miss the intricate details of the anatomy lesson.

Her partner's request brought a smile to Radha's lips. "*I myself am not sure what is ailing me, I am only too happy to honor Kamala's request for distance as it gives me an excuse to just sit and watch the procedures, and am especially thankful not to be using any sharp blades and instruments, right now!*"

Radha said aloud, "I really appreciate your concern. I don't feel very good and am glad you can carry on with the dissection without my help. Thank you." For the time being she had escaped further scrutiny by her friends.

Biochemistry lab sessions followed, which emitted as much hot air from the professor as from the Bunsen burners in the laboratory, and left her in a daze most of the day.

Radha had to attend introductory patient rounds, which meant that she had to go to the hospital inpatient buildings, which were a mile away from the College campus. On the days when the lab practicums ran late, if she missed the shuttle bus, she ended up walking to the hospital. To arrive late for 'rounds', was pure torture, because the senior students and residents loved to pick on any juniors that were in the least bit conspicuous. It was a true juggling act to stay out of trouble from them. It was as if she was caught in the wheels of a merry-go-round gone wild! There was no stopping until 8 or 9 at night.

On Tuesday, her father called, "Radha, I'll send the car for you at 7 p.m. Come and have dinner with me, and

I'll drop you back at the Hostel later in the evening." It had become routine that she joined her father for dinner on Tuesdays, unless she had a class scheduled that conflicted with such plans. That particular Tuesday, although there was no such conflict she did not feel up to her father's scrutiny. "There is a major test in Anatomy on Friday. I better stay back today, achan." She made her excuses.

At last Saturday arrived, and by early afternoon her patient rounds were over and she was back at her hostel. As soon as she walked into the building she heard Kamala's voice calling out to her over the top of the din in the foyer, which was packed full with many of her colleagues. "Radha, we are going to see the Clark Gable movie, Teacher's Pet. Join us, and we can even stop by Xavier's for ice-cream first, before the Theater. The College Van will pick us up at 3 p.m. Be ready."

"I don't feel up to it, Kamala," Radha's voice was meek and elusive, and she could not look Kamala straight in the eye. "I'm staying back tonight."

"You're going to miss a fun trip," Kamala was persistent.

"Come on Radha," Indira chimed in. "When have you been too tired to see a Clark Gable movie? You must be terminally ill!" Everyone laughed. Radha's cheeks burned red.

Radha did not give in. To her relief the college van pulled off with her dear but loud friends at 3 p.m. sharp.

Radha left word at the *Mess Hall,* or Cafeteria, to hold a late supper. She then picked up her book of poems by Tagore and walked the half-mile or so to the College grounds. She felt an urgency to get away from the demanding daily routine and the noises she had normally tolerated, but which now seemed unbearable. Walking briskly, her curly hair wantonly blowing around her lovely face, a spectator would wonder why such a young face

carried such a forlorn, worried expression. But how she
looked to others was the farthest thing from Radha's mind.
She wanted to get to a secluded spot in the garden behind
the main college building. As she passed by the long
hedgerows of magenta and white bougainvilleas, she
noticed how as they danced in the light breeze, they caught
the bright rays of the afternoon sun and their petals
sparkled like jewels by a shining lamp. The sight of the
bright blossoms lifted her spirit slightly and her steps lost
some of the tense pounding, slowing her to more of a
leisurely stroll as she neared the College grounds.

The walk took her around the fields where a dozen
or so students were still batting at Cricket, which was
really a little late for a Saturday afternoon, and then past
the Tennis courts. She found herself searching for Danny's
face among the players, and the realization made her blush.
She could not fathom why. She saw that he was not there.

Radha was known to be a levelheaded one, one who
usually had her life in perfect control. Growing up
motherless, the daughter of a highly respected, highly-
placed judge in town, she was never prone to any teen-age
frivolities. Her father, Judge Unnikrishna Menon was one
for strict discipline. After her Amma's death, Radha had
felt an innate feeling of responsibility for her actions and
for her father's wellbeing. She was determined not
jeopardize her father's peace of mind or his social status.
After the initial shock of losing her mother to a short tragic
illness, Radha had depended on Ammini-Ammavi, Aunt
Ammini, who dropped in regularly and was truly her
surrogate mom. Ammini-Ammavi had never had any
occasion to reprimand or discipline Radha. Ammini-
Ammavi had a relaxed fun-loving personality and Radha
enjoyed visiting her often, since her house was only a few
minutes walk from Radha's. Ammini-Ammavi had raised
three of her own, all of whom were older than Radha,

married or moved on with their own lives, leaving
Ammini-Ammavi with abundant time to cater to Radha's
needs. She was an older cousin of Radha's mother, and
having grown up together in an extended matriarchal
family, she had known Radha's mother very well. Ammini-
Ammavi told her stories of her own mother that Radha as a
young girl would have otherwise forgotten.

So, past the tennis courts Radha went, to the garden
behind the Medical College. By now the sun's rays were
turning to evening gold and slantingly casting shadows of
tall Cyprus trees that waved gently in the evening breeze.
They appeared to Radha like old withered friends waving
their hands in welcome, inviting her to her favorite spot of
respite from the busy world of bodies, living and dead. The
sweet and mildly intoxicating smell of jasmines in bloom
soothed her heart, a heart that had carried such unusual
turbulence within it for the past week. The lush green grass
of the well-tended lawn felt especially soft underfoot. Her
weary body and soul felt a sense of relief as she settled
under a shady Mango tree with her cherished book of
poetry "*Gitanjali*," Song Offerings. Radha was especially
pleased that her close friends were at the movies and
would not intrude on her quiet moments with her favorite
poet.

There she was deep in the solace of the magical
words of Tagore, when she heard footsteps behind her and
turning her head around, she saw him approaching. There
was no place for her to hide, the vast gardens offered no
buildings close enough to walk into, and, why did she feel
she wanted to escape from him? She could not have
escaped anyway, her body and her feet felt weak and
suddenly immobile.

"Maya," he uttered softly. There was no light
glibness in Danny's voice unlike when they first met, when
that name was a jovial pronouncement on his part. "I was

hoping to find you here. I have repeatedly tried to call you and even waited outside your physiology class one day last week to talk to you."

"Why?" Radha asked innocently. Danny was silent. Even as she asked the question, her heart saw the answer in his eyes. The realization sent a wave of unbearable warmth, no heat, through her pulses. The air was heavy with the silence, and she was afraid to move for fear of what would happen next.

After what seemed to her an interminable minute, the nearby rustle of leaves told her that he had sat down beside her.

"It has been one week since we met at the Kovalam beach, and when you left the verandah of the Kovalam Palace, you took my life with you. I have not been able to function normally since that day. Maya, I cannot get you out of my mind." Danny's words did not surprise her.

Radha looked up, saw the longing in his eyes and looked away again. She was afraid that in another moment her eyes would give away her feelings. How was she going to tell him she felt the same way, without creating a situation she knew both of them would regret?

The year was 1965 and she knew they were of a liberated age and time in a free India, but any discussion of their feelings would have to be tempered by the fact they were of two different religions, she a Hindu, of a Nair caste, whereas he was a Christian, a Catholic. Radha knew that although her father would not oppose to letting her wed a man of her choice, the lines were very clearly drawn as to whom she could marry. To get her father's blessings she would have to choose a young man who was a Hindu, preferably of a Nair caste, and definitely a professional with conventional leanings. Danny certainly did not fit the bill, on any of those counts. For Radha to get involved in anything more than a mere friendship with Danny was courting disaster, of that she was well aware.

He moved closer, picked up her book and with surprising familiarity turned to page ninety-two, and proceeded to read aloud:

"I love you beloved. Forgive me my love.
Like a bird losing its way I am caught.
When my heart was shaken it lost its veil and was naked.
Cover it with pity, beloved, and forgive me my love.
If you cannot love me, beloved, forgive me my pain
Do not look askance at me from far
I will steal back to my corner and sit in the dark
With both hands I will cover my naked shame
Turn your face from me, my beloved, and forgive me my pain
If you love me, beloved, forgive me my joy.
When my heart is borne away by the flood of happiness,
do not smile at my perilous abandonment
When I sit on my throne and rule you with my tyranny of love,
When like a goddess I grant you my favor, bear with my pride, beloved, and forgive me my joy."

He closed the book and placed his right hand on her left, and faced her.

"Maya, I know what you are thinking. I am a Catholic, albeit a non-practicing one and you are an ardent Hindu girl." He paused. "I am fully aware that anything you say from now on is a commitment. We may regret this, but whether I put it in so many words or not, my commitment is made, and there is no way that I can live without you. I love you Maya, and that's all there is to it."

Radha turned her face towards him, it was impossible to hide it even if she wanted to, "I, I feel the same way, too. Oh Danny! What are we going to do? You know that I come from a very orthodox Hindu family. Any commitment I make to you would be betraying my father, and I'm all that he has."

Danny placed a soft finger on her lips. "Shh.... Maya dear. Now that I know how you feel, I can think straight. We will come up with some solution."

"We cannot talk here." Radha stood up and glanced toward other walkers who passed by. "Tomorrow after morning patient rounds, I'll see you in the Medicine department waiting room. Being Sunday, the staff will not be there."

"Okay," he said, "I'm on cloud nine, and can breathe again. But I know I'll not sleep a wink!" And then he was gone.

She realized then he had called her 'Maya'. Never once had he called her Radha. She smiled. Yes, it was a make-believe world that they were in. The sun was setting, and it would be dark soon in the real world. Her pounding heart caused ripples in her vision and she could not read any more. She hugged her book tightly to her bosom and headed back to her room.

Radha was elated by the surge of new and glorious feelings welling within her. She saw her smiling face in the mirror. As she gazed, her smile was replaced by a frown, and her shoulders drooped. How would she follow her heart and yet avoid pain for her father? Her thoughts were interrupted by a knock on her door.

She rubbed the frown off her face and opened her door. It was Naani Amma from the kitchen. Radha dreaded a lecture from Naani Amma for missing her supper. But, apparently, Naani Amma understood. There she stood with a cup of hot cocoa.

"Radha-môl", she said. "I thought you might be coming down with a cold or something when I heard that you had cancelled your supper. Maybe you could use a cup of hot cocoa?"

Naani Amma had a soft spot for the motherless sixteen year old, who was one of the sweetest in the crowd. She placed the cocoa on the table, and closed the door. Turning around, she grasped both of Radha's shoulders, and spoke. "I know it is no cold that is bothering you. I have watched you for the past week. You have not been eating well, and you have not been talking to me either. All this is since your trip to Kovalam. Tell me what happened, and maybe I can help you."

Radha was defenseless in front of this pure unconditional affection, and all her barriers broke down. "I can't tell you what happened, because I myself don't know what is happening to me."

Radha sat down on her bed, and Naani Amma pulled up a chair and sat across from her. She would not sit on the bed with Radha, of course. As close as they had become, she still was an employee while Radha was a resident of the hostel. She took both Radha's hands in hers and said, "kunjé, child," I have seen a few aching hearts myself and know that yours is one right now. Let me help you."

Radha looked into Naani Amma's eyes and searched into the depths of her own heart to see if she should confide in her. She followed her instincts and said, "last week I met this young man at the outing at Kovalam. I think I have fallen in love with him and he told me today that he loves me too!"

"So, what is the problem then? Who is he?" Naani Amma interrupted. Radha swallowed hard.

"He is a Christian boy, a Catholic to be exact - and you know how that would go over with my father!"

"Oh!" Naani Amma took a deep breath. "That definitely poses a problem."

Both sat quietly for a while. Naani Amma's voice was firm, when she finally spoke. "Kunjé, I have seen so many Nair relationships that are miserable that I am not sure that religion has to play any part in any human relationship. Religion is between a man and God. No other human being has to come between that. But my philosophy is not the issue at hand! I need to help you handle your problem. I don't have any answers. But one thing I do know. There is no gain in getting yourself sick over this. Drink your cocoa. Take a warm shower and go to bed. You say your prayers and I'll say mine. Between the two of us and the almighty God we will certainly come up with some solution." She hugged Radha tight, and left the room, closing the door quietly behind her.

Radha pulled her weary body out of bed and slowly sipped on the cocoa. The hot liquid in her stomach seemed to soothe away some of the tightness in her chest. Naani Amma was right.

She showered, changed her clothes and returned to her room for her evening prayers. Hindu tradition called for a fresh clean body and a clear mind prior to prayers. She lit an oil lamp, the formless flickering flame and the light it sheds symbolizing the ubiquitous power of Narayana, The Lord of the Universe. She wearily sat down to her ritual of pooja and prayers. Her usual chants of prayers started with one for Lord Ganesha, the elephant headed one, the one who would get rid of all obstacles. *"Ganesha sharanam, sharanam Ganesha,"* I surrender to your grace, Ganesha, she chanted.

"Oh Ganesha! even you cannot tear this wall of obstacles down," she said out loud, as sobs interrupted her chanting and the familiar words of her prayers escaped her fumbled mind.

She took a deep breath, closed her eyes and resumed her chanting. *"Krishna Krishna~ Mukunda~Janardana~,"* she addressed Lord Krishna by all his glorified names, pleading for help to get her out of the predicament she was in. Lord Krishna's advice to prince Arjuna, (who flounders when faced with having to fight his own kith and kin in a battle of good versus evil) is the essence of the Bhagavad Geetha, the Lord's song, which is considered as the Hindu Bible. But tonight Radha was too far gone in her misery to continue or complete her daily prayers. The confusion in her mind made her feel that saying her prayers was an exercise in futility. Where was the power of prayer when she needed it most?

Chapter Three
Amma, Mother

> *This song of mine will wind music around you, my child,*
> *like the fond arms of love.... ....*
> *And when my voice is silent in death,*
> *my song will speak in your living heart...*
>   *Rabindranath Tagore*

The evening sun cast long shadows on the window, as her Amma lit the lamp in her pooja room and placed garlands of chrysanthemums on the idols of Lord Krishna and Ganesha. That day, she had allowed Radha to help make the garlands, showing the young girl how to use the string from a banana plant to tie the knots around the delicate stems of the flowers, as she wove the garlands. At six years of age, Radha knew it was a special honor that she was allowed to help make the garlands. She looked up from where she sat in front of the lamp, and smiled to see the jasmines that she had woven on her Amma's glistening hair, still wet from her recent bath. Amma always took a bath and changed into fresh clothes before her evening prayers. Amma said prayers all the time, but at dusk they were very special. "It is the time when the day is over, and we have to thank the Lord for all our blessings," her Amma had said. "It is also the time when the light of the sun gives way to the darkness of the night, and we need to ask protection of the Lord from the dangers in the dark." The sweet smell of the jasmines and the mums mingled with the aroma of the incense sticks, and wafted up to put them in a relaxed, soft mood, as Amma started her chanting. When Radha repeated a favorite chant of Amma's that she had just mastered, Amma turned to her, her eyes glowing with pride. At the conclusion of her evening prayers, Amma lit pieces of sweet smelling camphor in a brass holder, and let the smoke envelope the idols. The offering of the fire, she explained to her little girl, was an act that symbolized surrendering our problems at the Lord's feet for caretaking. The burning flame got rid of any bad thoughts we have, and also burnt away bad karma at the same time.

Radha opened her eyes and realized she was dreaming. She sat up in her bed, weeping silently. Memories of Amma were clear at times, but blurred scenes from the past confused her sometimes, and she was not certain they really occurred. Often the stories that her Ammini Ammavi had told her fused with pictures of what she really remembered of her time with her Amma, like the time she had asked about the Hindu religion. "Why do we have statues to worship? My friend Lily says that there are no statues at the altar in the Church that she goes to. And, Amma, how come we go to the Temple on all different days? Lily only goes to church on Sundays. "

"We are Hindus and we believe that the power known as Yeshwara, God, is formless like the flame of the lamp," Amma answered, "periodically, such power descends to this bhoomi, the earth, to get rid of evils and to help the good people, and that is when Yeshwara takes forms that are visible to us called avatars. We pray to those avatars, the various incarnations that God appeared in, on this bhoomi. To make it easy for us to pray to the Lord, we idolize these forms as they appear to us. Lord Krishna is my favorite avatar," she had proclaimed.

Lord Krishna was Radha's favorite, too. She had loved sitting by her mother's side as she chanted verses from Bhagavatham, the book from which Amma read all the stories of the ten avatars of Lord Vishnu. She could not really understand all the stories or their significance, but the sight of Amma's face, enraptured in the songs and verses that she chanted to invoke Krishna's blessings, was so serene and beautiful that Radha did not even think of questioning the deeper meaning of the prayers, nor of the rituals. For that matter, none of her friends did then, either.

"Why do we have to pray to Ganesha first if your favorite is Krishna?" Radha had asked her Amma at one time.

"That is because Ganesha is the god in charge of keeping any obstacles away. So we propitiate Him first." Amma answered, smiling kindly.

"What does propitiate mean?" Radha continued.

Amma smiled. "You are a curious one, aren't you? Well, it means to do things to please someone in order to get their help. And when we please Ganesha, the elephant-headed one, he smoothes our way through everyday rituals and any new projects that we undertake, without any problems."

————

Her thoughts about her Amma were interrupted by more thoughts about Danny. Why did the fact that Danny was a Christian torment her and keep her from pursuing her feelings about him? And how did she really feel about him? Why did she have a hard time saying her prayers and even doing her pooja rituals, earlier that evening? She had more questions than answers. And this time, Amma was not there to answer them.

Radha had learned to pray at her Amma's knees. She also learned all about her religion from Amma. Later in life, she had heard it said that Hinduism is a way of life, not just a religion. The way her Amma practiced Hinduism was more than just a way of life. It was her whole life! There was no waking moment in her life that her mother did not think of God. "Swamee, rakshikkané, " Oh Lord, please take care (of us), her Amma uttered any time she ventured out of her house, and even when Radha set out for school everyday. It was a phrase constantly at her Amma's lips. Radha came to believe that in invoking Swami, The Lord, she would automatically gain His blessing and support in everything she did.

It was also in the pooja room that she learned of all the different festivals. Each special occasion called for its own special food. For Krishna's birthday they made oonniappams, special banana fritters made with ripe bananas, rice flour and brown sugar. At pooja time, the oonniappams were placed in offering in front of the oil lamp. Even Radha was only allowed to taste any of them after the pooja was over. For that matter any special food ever prepared was first offered to Ganesha, to be blessed, before anybody could partake of it. Amma had implicit faith in the effects of her prayers and offerings, and never wavered in her practices. And so, too, Radha loved and trusted her Amma implicitly.

"I wish she were here to make oonniappams for me, now. " Radha mumbled as she fell into a restless sleep.

Amma combed Radha's hair, as they were getting ready to go to the temple. She chanted a prayer as she combed and braided Radha's hair into a long ponytail. At the temple her mother stood in front of their favorite deity, Lord Krishna, while Radha roamed around the temple yard with the nanny, so that her Amma could pray in peace. It was a lovely sight to see her Amma enraptured in prayer, eyes half-closed, her lips moving in prayer, but without any discernible sounds emanating from them. Her palms were joined together with upturned fingers and Radha felt a sense of peace. She was confident that her Amma's prayers kept her and her father safe from all worldly woes.

Radha woke up with a start. She sat up and turned the lights on in her small hostel room. Now she knew that her Amma's prayers had not really kept them safe. Where was Amma now?

When her Amma was alive, it had been a peaceful world. The greatest worry Radha had on any day was that she would not see her father before her bedtime. Unnikrishna Menon was a totally dedicated lawyer and his practice of the law was all consuming. Many were the nights that he went from court to the law library to do research for his defenses, or to a colleague's house for the long mock trials that they enacted to hone their skills for their day in court. On those nights, Radha did not see her achan before her bedtime. She remembered fondly the times when the law group held the sessions at her house. Her Amma worked extra hard to make the house look pretty... not that it was ever not pretty! She even let Radha carry the flowers in from the garden and help her arrange them in large groupings in every corner of the house. Kamalamma, the cook, would be busy all day preparing a delicious dinner. But what pleased Radha most were the many snacks that she prepared for the guests. Kamalamma allowed the young girl to help roll the special pastries that were then fried in hot oil, one by one. Radha knew well that the ones she rolled could not be served to the guests because they were not only imperfectly shaped, but many were totally out of shape! Radha sat munching them with her Amma while they waited for her father's colleagues to arrive. Many a time the attorneys' spouses accompanied them on those sessions, and it was at those times that Radha was thrilled to hear her Amma talk about how `my kochu-môl' helped her in the kitchen. Amma had a neat way of making her feel important. Radha could not remember ever being yelled at or put down by her Amma.

But all that ended on the day when Ammini-Ammavi picked her up at school and abruptly interrupted her classes.

Radha closed her eyes, and the events of that fateful day seemed like yesterday.

"Radha- môl, " even at the tender age of eight Radha had felt the urgency in Ammini-Ammavi's voice. "Your Amma had to be taken to the hospital for some tests, because she became ill very suddenly."

"Why did she have to go to the hospital for tests? Why won't the doctor come to the house to test her like he did when I had pneumonia?" Radha asked her Ammavi in the car on the way to the hospital.

"I really don't know why, my dear." Ammini-Ammavi said, in a hoarse voice.

At the hospital, it seemed like ages before they would let Radha see her mother. Radha looked up and saw that Ammini-Ammavi was crying. She was just about to ask why she was crying, when her achan walked into the room. Radha ran to him and grabbed his hand. He leaned down and kissed her on the top of her head. Then he hugged her tightly to him. She thought it was unusual that he hugged her for no obvious reason. He only did that on her birthday or when he was saying goodbye, before a long trip. Usually, a pat on her head and a squeeze of her cheeks were all she got from him when he came home.

In his usual demanding voice, achan asked to see the doctor who was taking care of his wife. Soon the doctor came to see him. He wore blue pants and a sleeveless blue top, which Radha found out later, were outfits doctors wore in the operating rooms. All of a sudden she felt scared, and she moved over and grabbed her achan's arm, and held on tight, as she listened to the doctor's words. "We have found a ruptured cyst in the right ovary. She has lost quite a bit of blood, and already we have given her blood transfusion to avoid her going into shock. We have to operate on her immediately."

Her achan hugged her closer.

Before the operation, Radha was allowed to go in and see her Amma. She appeared tired and weak and looked so pale on the crisp white sheets that for years Radha could not see white sheets on a bed without a shiver. Tubes with red blood and clear fluids were attached to her arms. She was drowsy, and her speech was slurred, as she raised her free arm and pulled Radha towards her in an effort to hug her. Radha remembered how, between her sobs and tears, she had mumbled, "Lord Krishna was going to make everything alright," and that, "you have to be strong for your father."

Since the operation took a long time, Radha was sent home with Ammini-Ammavi, who had sat by her bedside until Radha fell asleep.

The next morning her achan took Radha to see her Amma.

"Why are you not going to court today? Don't I have to go to school?" The interruption in her daily routine alarmed the young girl and she started to cry.

Her achan sat down beside her.

"Dear môl, don't cry." His voice was unusually soft. "I know that you don't understand this, but they have found out that your Amma has cancer. She had a big operation last night, and she will have to stay at the

hospital for a few more days. You and I will have to take
care of each other, okay?"

Now, years later, she remembered that all she had
understood was the ominous tone in his voice, and that the
words had offered no specific meaning that day.

The remaining time she had spent with Amma were
a hazy blur of repeated trips to the hospital where she was
allowed to see very little of her Amma. Her Amma could
not answer her questions, and could not even hold her
close or hug her, because she was so weak. Radha came
away with painful memories of her Amma crying in pain
as she tossed and turned restlessly in her hospital bed.

Then one day Amma seemed a little stronger. When
Radha entered the room, she motioned her to come closer,
and with feeble arms, gathered her to her side.

"Môl," Amma's voice was barely audible, and Radha
started to cry.

"Don't cry Radha- môl. I have to tell you something;
and I want you to listen very carefully. I have to go away
now, because my time on earth is over. I love you and your
achan very much and would like very much to stay with
you, but God does not want me to suffer anymore pain and
is going to take me to heaven. Now, I want you to be brave,
promise to remember that I love you. Take care of your
achan. Listen to Ammini Ammavi, say your prayers and do
your homework."

Ammini-Ammavi sobbed as she led Radha out of
the room, and Radha remembered how Judge Menon
asked her to "stop crying or you will upset the young girl."

Later the same day, crowds of family and friends
arrived, and they brought Amma's body and laid her out in
the front hall, on a straw mat, without any bedding, and
Radha ran up to her. She could not fathom why they did
not lay her on a bed, or at least a comforter, like the ones

Radha used on the floor to play dolls with. She ran up to her and picked up her Amma's hand.

"Amma, Amma, wake up. Get up and go to your bed to sleep." Suddenly Radha dropped Amma's hand. Why was it so cold?

She looked up with frightened eyes towards her achan. He looked back at her sternly and she did not feel he would welcome any questions from her. She ran to her Ammini Ammavi, who sat crying in a corner of the room.

"Ammini Ammavi, who gave Amma a bath? She smells so good, and why is she all dressed up? Where is she going?"

Ammini Ammavi wiped her tears and led her by her Amma's body. She sat down, gathered Radha on to her lap and spoke directly to her. "Môl, your Amma is with Yeshwara, now. It is only her body that is here with us, and she cannot talk to you any more. She will always hear you and look out for you from heaven. We have to stop crying and both of us shall say prayers for her soul to leave in peace."

Radha could not quite understand all that was said, but when Ammini-Ammavi and some others ladies started chanting of prayers, Radha stopped crying and huddled by Ammini-Ammavi.

Later, they covered Amma's body with white and red drapes of cloth, and one by one the friends and relatives went around the still body and laid flowers on her. Achan held Radha's hand and led her up to the still figure, and gave her some rose petals to place on Amma's forehead. Radha saw the pale face and started screaming. Ammini-Ammavi took her from her achan to the farther end of the room, and consoled and calmed her.

Then, four of the men picked up her Amma, and carried her out of the house.

Radha could not understand why they had to take her Amma away. Ammini-Ammavi had fainted, and Radha could not get any answers to her many questions. She was not allowed to go with her Amma to the 'cremation grounds' She realized that she would not see her Amma anymore.

———————

"If my Amma were alive, I probably would be still living at home, attending Medical school as a day scholar, and definitely would not have gone to the Kovalam picnic." Radha mused. "Maybe it would have been better, because then I would not have to worry about my feelings for Danny, and the conflicts of our religions." She missed her Amma.

What would Amma say about her feelings for Danny? If she told her Amma that she was falling in love with this Christian boy, what would she say? Maybe she would tell Radha that, "in the eyes of Yeshwara, all human beings were equal, and that praying to God, whatever name you used to call Him by, (Vishnu, Krishna, or Jesus) did not matter." She would probably tell Radha that the important thing is that you have faith in the power of The Almighty. Radha was certain that even if Amma reminded her of being practical about the difficulties of a mixed marriage, she would be able to win her Amma over to her side, once Radha told her how much in love she was with her Danny.

But, for now it was an exercise in futility, since her Amma was not with her anymore.

Chapter Four

Hands cling to hands and eyes linger on eyes:
thus begins the record of our hearts... ...
This love between you and me is simple as a song...
    Rabindranath Tagore

The street lights were bright, yet the flames of the torches perched on the sides of the streets were truly blinding. A makeshift music band had taken over the side-walk. Loud drums balanced rhythmic percussion on the kaddam, a ceramic water jar-like instrument, and a husband-wife pair bellowed out folk songs. The flashy colors of the man's baggy pants, a mixture of orange, red and brilliant yellow were outmatched by her bright pink choli blouse over an ultramarine blue skirt and a semi-transparent yellow scarf tied at the waist, both of which swayed with her full hips as her body moved to the words of her folk songs. They set the mood on the street, where Radha found herself dancing in the arms of Danny, alongside Kamala, Soman, and others who were at the Kovalam beach picnic.

Everyone stopped moving. A mourning song from the woman singer, accompanied by melancholy strains from a violin which appeared out of nowhere in the hand of her male partner, replaced their dance music and the sounds of the drums.

Radha turned around and saw Danny at the other end of the street, waving her goodbye. She tried to run towards him.

*But, there was a wave of bodies between them, as the entire crowd
was leaving in haste, and preventing her from reaching him.*

Radha woke up in a sweat. "Why am I dreaming of
saying goodbye to Danny when I have barely said hello?"
Radha said out loud, to herself. It did not make any sense.
She wanted to say more than hello to Danny, yet her
pragmatic doctor-side told her that she was approaching a
danger zone. She stood up and was forced to grab the edge
of her bed to steady herself. Her head was spinning.

No time to be dizzy now, she said to herself as she
wearily pulled herself together and went on to make the
medicine rounds. She had promised to meet Danny after
rounds. She made it through the morning without any
incidents. Much to her immense relief, when she entered
the Department of Medicine waiting room, it was empty.
She did not have to wait long. The doors opened abruptly,
and in walked Danny. He laid his stethoscope on the table
and sauntered over to her. She was stunned to see the glow
in his eyes set off by the sun, and again her heart melted
like butter. She felt the heat of his love. He reached up and
took her in his arms. It was the first time that a man held
her so. She was too weak to resist, even if she wanted to.
Tentatively, hesitantly, his lips brushed hers.

"No! no!" She moved away. No, she could not give
in to his passion or her own.

Danny turned and sat down at the table, and buried
his head in his hands.

She walked over and took a chair across from him.

"Danny, I...I don't know what to say. I want very
much to love you." She stammered. "My body aches with
love for you, but I...I really don't feel right about it. I cannot
betray my achan. I cannot jeopardize my future as a doctor.
By giving in to my wants and emotions now, I will be
shattering an old man's dreams. I cannot build our

dreamcastle on the ruins of my achan's. Not now. Not ever!" Her voice faltered and her eyes stayed fixed on the table. She could not face Danny.

The sunlight disappeared as clouds moved into the sky and darkened the room reflecting the mood they were drifting into.

Danny leaned over and grasped her shoulders, and looked straight into her eyes. "Maya," he was using his special name for her again, "there has to be a solution to this problem. I am not giving up, even before we give this love of ours a chance."

His hands on her shoulders felt like hot rods of lightning and they lit up her whole body in a passion that she had never experienced before. At nineteen, she was young, but not naive. She did not recognize the strength of her feelings for him, but knew that she was entering a danger zone. Her mouth was dry, her palms moist and she could feel her heart ready to burst within her bosom, it was beating so fast. Innately her mind told her to take action. She stood up and, shaking his hands off her shoulders, turned, and began to walk away from him. But, a power greater than her disciplined mind tugged at her whole being, and pulled her back and into his arms. Lips touched and pressed hard. They were in an embrace so tight that for many moments they could not breathe. Nevertheless, there seemed to be no urgency to breathe anymore. The power of the passion that held them together was a life in itself, breathing on its own. She felt they would never move again.

After what seemed to be an eternity, Danny moved, and tenderly lifting her radiant face just inches away from his, her body still prisoner within his embrace, stood gazing into her eyes.

"Maya, I don't want you to do anything you are not happy about. We can see each other and just enjoy each other's company. We don't have to make any lifelong promises today. Just promise me I can see you after classes tomorrow."

"Danny," she whispered," I can't say no, although I know I should. I shall meet you after classes at the same place you found me reading yesterday." She picked up her books and walked out before he had a chance to speak.

The tomorrow she spoke of turned out to be a glorious day. The warm sunshine seemed to bring out the best in nature that afternoon, when Danny came to meet Radha under the stately palms behind the Medical College Buildings. Bougainvilleas waved their welcomes in the soft breeze. Cyprus trees swung their soft lacy branches in a special effort to cool them from the hot sun. Jasmines opened up the best of their buds and smiled warmly to welcome them to this special place of retreat, enveloping them in a strong fragrance that made them giddy, conducive to making even tough old men soft inside. One can only imagine what it did to two souls madly in love, and at that a forbidden one!

"Look at my favorite birds," Radha pointed to the two hummingbirds busily circling the Jasmines. "They are so busy playing; they are not even drinking of the honey in the open blossoms."

"Don't you see, they are also in love! Let us take their lead. Let us have a great time together and pretend the rest of the world does not exist."

Danny turned towards Radha and took her hands in his, drawing her towards him. "You are the most beautiful woman I have ever seen in my life. All the glory of this garden pales in the light of your beauty. It makes me feel I have been asleep for the past two decades of my life and just awoke to see all that is worthwhile in life." He let go of her hands and ran his fingers through his hair in his usual thinking mode.

"You know how busy I have been, protesting every little inequity in life." He stopped fidgeting with his hair, faced her squarely and continued. "Now, I don't feel like sharing you with the rest of the world. I know that is not fair. But this is one inequity I do want to tolerate! I want to take you away, make you mine and mine alone, retire to a high mountain top and spend my entire life gazing into your beautiful eyes. The sound of your voice to quench my thirst and the sight of your smiling face are all the food I need to thrive on for the remainder of my mortal life."

Radha's cheeks turned a crimson hue matching the colors of the low evening sun. "Oh, Danny! No one has ever said such beautiful words to me. But," she added in protest, "I think the warmth of this sun, the sounds of the Koil birds singing and the fragrance of the jasmines bursting with their warm honey, are getting to you, and making you say things you don't mean. I am sure when your head returns to the ground from its flight of fancy into those billowy clouds of your imagination, you will not feel the way you do now."

"How can you say that? Don't be so cavalier about my feelings, please. You know very well it was my blunt sincerity that landed me in trouble with the College authorities, more than once." Danny stopped and he was fingering his hair again. Radha knew he was nervous.

"I take great pride in my honesty, and believe me when I say I love you. Those words may have been used by many before me, but none have come close to the truth compared to how I feel about you. I wish I had more unique words to express how I feel about you."

Quickly moving closer to her, he opened his arms to her. She reached up to him, and naturally, effortlessly fell into them in a tight embrace. No words were spoken. A silent pact was sealed in front of God and nature, by two hearts united by the purest of feelings known to mankind.

Like many before them, they knew not where it would take
them, but in the lack of wisdom of impetuous youth, they
sealed their bond with a kiss. The birds sang loud and
nature rejoiced with them, in this, their grandest moment
in life.

Thus started a relationship filled with blissful walks
on the beach, music-filled evenings under moonlit skies
and vacation spots stolen under the guise of field trips. The
field trips were often required as part of their curriculum
and hence never questioned by their families. They stayed
away from tourist-trodden paths for fear of meeting
mutual acquaintances. They stole away from their
respective groups, separately, to then meet under stately
columns of coconut trees and the lush greenery of oleander
hedges in bloom.

On occasion they even braved their colleagues' eyes
to go to a Saturday night movie at the Campus Greens and
managed to sit close enough to hold hands when the lights
were out. When beautiful maidens danced on the movie
screen, Danny told her how she was ten times more
beautiful than any one of them. When lovers pledged their
lives and love to each other, Danny was the first to note
that their promises were of very little significance
compared to his pledge to her, and reminded her of the
wonderful life, filled with fun and laughter that they
would share. When babies were born to the hero and
heroine of the stories that they watched, he promised that
their offspring would be adorable and adored, more than
any cinema screen could portray!

"Danny, no! don't tease me, please," she would
protest when he waxed poetic in praise of her good looks.

"Do you mean to tell me you don't trust my ability to
appreciate beauty when I see it?" He would pretend to be
offended. "I love you, my dear Maya, and if that is a crime,
I'll gladly accept all the punishment you mete out to me."

Despite their original resolve not to make any commitments for the future, they found themselves planning a future in which their children would bring both their families together, for what grandfather could resist the face of his own progeny, knowing the young faces would assure his immortality in this world?

It was on those out of town field trips they really bared their souls to each other. Many were the nights that they sat on the sands of the beach at Kovalam, holding hands and discussing a happy future together. While the radio hummed tunes of romances gone awry, they promised that would not happen to them.

"Somehow we will find a solution to our problem. Let us not spoil our times together worrying about our religious differences, now." Danny said vehemently, when Radha brought up the subject. They knew that as much as they tried to ignore it, it loomed as a dark cloud on the distant horizon.

Meanwhile, Naani Amma was the only soul Radha confided in.

"Kunjé," she chided Radha. "When are you coming down to earth? The heavenly bliss that you now feel has to withstand the scrutiny of practical life; the stark sunlight of reality would soon fade this bliss away if we don't find a solution, soon."

"We want to put off the worries of an impossible future for the time being and enjoy our time together to the fullest extent possible." Radha justified herself to Naani Amma.

Naani Amma shook her head in dismay. "You have said this for two years now, and pretty soon Danny has to make up his mind about the Residency training in Surgery." She put a loving arm on Radha's shoulder. "You, môl, have another year before you can graduate and anything you decide will have to be tempered by the fact you cannot jeopardize that."

Radha shared the conversation with Danny later the same evening. "It is a no win situation." She sadly admitted to Danny. "Our religious differences seem insurmountable. Achan will say, as long you follow the Christian faith, I cannot marry you."

"How about if I talk to him myself and assure him you will always remain a Hindu and promise him I will not interfere with your practicing Hinduism?"

"It is not just a matter of my practicing Hinduism. Achan has always wanted to have my marriage ceremony at his favorite Krishna temple at Guruvayoor in front of God and all our family and friends. You know that at Guruvayoor temple non-Hindus are not even allowed inside the main temple grounds! That is one more problem that he is having to face. Right or wrong, I am certain he believes my marrying out of caste would be demeaning to him and to our family."

Many were the discussions about their future or lack of hopes for one, and most often it ended up in the topic of her achan.

Chapter Five
Achan, Father

> *Let me not shame thee, Father, who displayest*
> *thy glory in thy children... ... ...*
> *Rabindranath Tagore*

Radha wished very much she could tell her achan about her love for Danny. But, how could she?

Radha knew her achan was different from all her friends' fathers. Her memories were vivid from when she was a young girl and her Amma was still alive. If Judge Menon, her achan, was around, he demanded all of her Amma's time and attention. As soon as he returned from court, Amma brought him tea and snacks, and Madhu, the young boy who was the cook's assistant, brought him his special house-slippers. Radha was only allowed to approach her achan when he called for her. Many a time, in her girlish exuberance she would race up to him, but her Amma would gently hold her back till she herself tested the waters, so to speak, and made sure her father was in a mood to deal with the young girl's energy and her chatter.

"Amma, why can't I go to achan and tell him about the puppies that my friend Geetha's dog gave birth to?" Radha remembered the time she questioned her Amma.

She had wanted one of those puppies very badly. But her Amma stopped her from asking achan for it.

"Your achan had a hard day at Court and should not be disturbed with such silly news." Amma explained.

"You had a hard day too, Amma." Radha had replied. "Ever since you came back from the temple this morning you have been working in the kitchen making all our favorite foods, and I know you are tired too! You don't tell me not to bother you if I want to come and talk or play with you."

"It is different with me", her Amma said, hugging her close. "I have the fun part of the job. Your achan has to deal with all sorts of difficult people all day, but I am lucky I get to be with you and have the satisfaction of seeing you eat and grow to be a smart, beautiful young lady."

Radha was quite tickled to be addressed as a young lady.

Although her Amma's comments distracted her temporarily, it still bothered her that her achan did not consider her as important as his work in court.

———

After her Amma passed away, her achan had changed. Radha remembered how instead of coming home at all odd and late hours in the law library, he came home early, every day.

"How come you are not staying late at the library any more?" She queried."

"I will do my reading at home after you go to bed. I want to see you learn your lessons with Ammini-Ammavi, and I want to hear you chant your evening prayers with her. Also, I want to make sure that Kamalamma cooks all your favorite dishes so that you will grow up strong."

Once, out of the corner of her eyes, Radha saw him wipe off a tear when he thought she wasn't watching. She was deeply affected by it. She realized that, although he had trouble showing his feelings for her, he really felt lonely for her late Amma, and in his own way he was trying to make sure Radha was not too lonely for her Amma.

Radha started hanging around her achan more often even if he did not always include her in what he was doing. Her instinct told her he needed her more than he would admit.

———————

She was curious about his childhood and about his life with her Amma. To her surprise he evaded all her queries about them. So she turned to Ammini-Ammavi to learn more about her achan.

"You see Radha-mol, even before he became a judge, your achan was autocratic and opinionated. When he married your Amma, he insisted on her quitting her job as a school-teacher to stay home and cater to him. She taught Malayalam, her favorite language, at the local high school and wished to keep on teaching after her marriage. But, 'no wife of mine needs to work outside the house to support me,' your achan said. He was also adamant she should be waiting for him at home when he returned from court every evening." Radha started to get glimpses of who he was.

Ammini-Ammavi went on to tell Radha more about her achan.

Judge Unnikrishnan Menon was of the old school. He had been raised with really old-fashioned, unbendable rules of moral and social conduct, by a very strict landowner father.

"His first memory of his father was the loud summons at daybreak that announced time to get up and go to school, at the local Guru's home. In the early days when Unnikrishnan was a little boy, schools as we know now did not exist in the small farming village of Manganam."

Ammini-Ammavi continued to fill in Radha about how her father hated the way his own father had treated him.

"Unnikrishna~--", his father had a long drawn emphasis to the way he called out for his son, when he demanded anything from him. When he was a young boy it confused him that his father never addressed him as "Unni," which was what his Amma called him, a short endearment of his name. When he got older and somewhat bolder, he asked his father why he never called him just Unni.

"You would be surprised at what your Appooppan, grandfather, said to him, then." Ammini-Ammavi continued. 'For a young man of the prestigious Kalaripparambil house to be addressed by anything less than his full name is a sign of disrespect, and I will not demean you by calling you by any short version of your given name.' His father was firm.

There was such a finality to the statement that it made Unnikrishnan straighten his back, hold his head high and even feel disdainful to his own mother's endearments, when she called him Unni. Ammini-Ammavi sighed sadly, as she sat on the front steps one sunny afternoon, combing Radha's long curly hair.

"Your achan has admitted to me and your Amma how he resented having to be under the thumb of such a strict disciplinarian, but I think some of it rubbed off on your achan himself, because he was impossible to live with when he was younger..."Ammini-Ammavi's voice trailed off, and Radha realized that the memories still upset her.

"You don't have to tell me anymore," Radha's voice was soft.

"No, no. It's all right. I just miss your Amma so much. She was not just my cousin. She was my best friend." Ammini-Ammavi wiped a tear off her cheek, as she continued.

"After they got married, your achan bought this house for your Amma, and she loved the big yard so she could plant and prune to her hearts content. She and I made plans to visit often, because my house is only two blocks away, as you well know. A few days after their marriage, your Amma came over to my house to visit while your father was in court. When he came home and found out where she was, he walked over to my house and ordered her to go back home. He followed her silently. As soon as they got home he yelled at her for leaving the house without his permission and expressly forbid her to do that again. It made your Amma sad, but then I came over here more often, and she made sure she had his permission the next time she came to visit me."

"And did he give her permission to come over and see you?"

"Yes, Radha-mol. He did give her permission to come over if she asked him. Don't worry mol, he was good to her otherwise." Radha realized that she must have seen the confusion in Radha's eyes. She quickly added. "No. no. He did not hit her or abuse her."

"You know Radha, dear. He has really changed since your Amma died. Do you remember how late he stayed out with his case-discussions, or at the law library? Now he is home for supper with you most of the time. Also, he talks to your teachers about your progress in school, and even asks my advice as to what type of clothes you need. I think you have really tamed the wild beast in him!"

Despite the change in her achan, Radha was still afraid of his displeasure, and tried not to do anything to upset him.

The first major crisis occurred when Radha completed the first two years of College and wished to apply for admission to Medical College.

Judge Menon wanted to look for an eligible bachelor for his daughter, in order to get her married off. It was customary that when young girls were of marrying age, inquiries were made for bachelors from respectable families. Once a young man with a sound education and prospects for a good future is located, an uncle or a family friend arranges to have the Horoscopes of the two people checked for compatibility. When such a compatible person is found, the prospective groom, his mother or an aunt, accompanied by an uncle, and perhaps a sister or a brother goes to the girl's house for 'pennukanal', which means to look over the girl. They would literally look her over, and if the girl met with their approval, then the young man was allowed to meet with her. In modern times, at least the young people were given the opportunity to meet and talk privately, and the girl is also given a choice to refuse a young man who is presented to her, if she was not pleased with him.

Radha was not ready to get married and 'settle down'. She wished to pursue a career in Medicine. She had a hard time convincing her achan she was serious about becoming a Doctor! She begged with Ammini-Ammavi to plead her case with him.

"Please tell him that after I finish Medicine, he can have all the pleasure of arranging my marriage. I need to become a doctor and help find a cure for the Cancer that killed my Amma. Also tell him I would be very miserable if he cut short my education now. This is something I have to do!" Radha was very convincing.

So Ammini-Ammavi ran interference for Radha. She explained to Judge Menon how important it was for his daughter to become a doctor. It was not easy. Ammini-Ammavi reminded him that after all Radha was only seventeen. Four and a half years, which was the duration of the Medical curriculum, was not too long to wait, before Radha got married and settled down. After constant pleading and coaxing on both their parts, they convinced him that a Doctor's profession was a very honorable one for a young lady. To Radha's relief, he relented, and she was free to pursue her dream.

Radha applied and was accepted as a medical student at The Trivandrum Medical College, only a few miles away from her home.

Now there was more conflict. Judge Menon insisted she stay at home and be a day scholar for the duration of the Medical curriculum.

"Achan, please be realistic." Radha had argued. "The trip to and from college would take more than an hour every day. It would be physically easier for me to live at the Women's Hostel on the College campus, and concentrate on my studies rather than waste time commuting on a daily basis."

"You are not going to stay in some dingy hostel room when you have such a comfortable room in this house of mine."

Radha saw his upper lip quiver, as he spoke, and he turned away from her. She realized he would miss her, but was not going to admit that was the real reason he did not want her to stay at the hostel.

She sat down beside him on the large sofa, and rested her head on his shoulder as she spoke. "Achan, dear, all you have to do is send the car for me whenever you want to see me. It really would make life easier if I stayed on Campus while I am in Medical school. Please, please say yes. I promise I will call you every night."

After repeated arguments, and some coaxing and cajoling, Judge Menon finally agreed to Radha moving to the women's hostel on the Medical College Campus.

The day before her move to the hostel, he threw a surprise party for Radha. As she and Kamala made plans for the room they were to share at the women's hostel, Ammini-Ammavi came up and nudged Radha to listen to what was going on behind her. They both heard Judge Menon brag to his friends, 'how his only daughter had blossomed into an independent young woman, and how proud he was of her.' Radha and Ammini Ammavi smiled at each other in disbelief. He would never say such things directly to her face.

———————

Now, three years later, here she was, wanting to tell him about her love for Danny.

Radha was on her weekly visit home, and she stood outside her achan's study practicing her lines.

Achan dear, I have fallen in love with this wonderful boy, Danny, and we wish to get married. He wants to come ask your permission for my hand, but he is a Christian. I want to assure you he will not try to convert me, and he will be very good for me. I also want you to know that I cannot live without him.

Through partly open doors, she saw her achan look up.

"Come on in Radha. What is on your mind?"

Radha walked in and stood by his armchair.

She lost her nerve.

"Nothing important. I see that you are busy with a case file. It can wait." That is all she could say.

So, Radha did not broach the subject of Danny with her achan.

Chapter Six

That which has the sanctions of ages,
have you the right to remove it?
  Rabindranath Tagore

Danny wanted to elope with Radha.

"No!" Radha's voice rose. "I cannot do that to my father. As much as I love you and want to spend the rest of my life with you, and as empty my life will be without you, I cannot do something so drastic that will hurt my father."

Danny was furious. "But, Radha, I cannot live without you anymore. What about our happiness?"

"Oh, Danny! We have a long life ahead of us. We really don't need to rush. I will not jeopardize my father's joy of celebrating an only daughter's graduation and a wedding he has dreamed of for a long time."

Many such arguments continued, but there was no solution in sight. "Maybe if you let me talk to him myself, I'll prove to him you mean more than my own life to me. He cannot resist that kind of logic." Danny pleaded with her.

"In good conscience Danny," she was firm, "I cannot place my father in a predicament as to choose between allowing me to marry a Christian and losing me. I am all he has in his life."

One night, when Radha returned home late from a movie, she found her father waiting up for her.

"Radha," his greeting was unusually abrupt, "I hear that you are seeing a young man?"

Radha was silent.

"I also hear from Dr. Poulose his name is Danny and he is a Christian!"

Radha nodded. So he had gotten the news from an unexpected source, Dr. Poulose, her biochemistry professor. Radha was not surprised. Everyone at the Medical College Campus knew about Danny and her, and she had known that it was only a matter of time before someone would break the news to her father.

"What is the meaning of this? How far do you intend to take this farce? As an only daughter of this Kalaripparambil house, how could you even think of taking up with such an upstart Christian boy?" Judge Menon continued.

"But Achâ!" she interrupted him gently but firmly, "I love Danny with all my heart. He loves me too. We are responsible adults, and we wish to get married. As for being an upstart Christian, I can guarantee you; he is more honest and respectable than many other young men of our religion I have come to know. And anyway what does that have to do with my happiness? Don't you want your only daughter to be happy?"

"How long do you think your happiness will last following a guitar-stringing bearded hippie doctor in his life-saving missions around the world, looking out for the poor and needy? What kind of life will he make for you, when he is thinking of others before you and your wellbeing?" He was shaking with anger. He had to stop talking and take a deep breath. "As for being a good Christian, I hear he does not even belong to any particular church!"

"Achâ!, you know very well being idealistic and helping people is a truer Christian act than going to church on Sundays." Radha moved close to her father, took both his hands in hers in a reconciliatory effort, and stated softly. "Danny has asked me to marry him!"

"Never!" He stood tall, towering above her. "Never while I am alive will I allow you to do that! You will not see him- this Danny-, anymore. I forbid you to mention his name in my presence!"

As he fumed out of the room, Radha saw him reach for a vial in his pocket and put a pill in his mouth. She had been aware he had some heart problems, and that he regularly saw his Cardiologist. God forbid he would confide in her. What she did not know was he carried the nitroglycerine pills with him all the time and his heart condition was serious enough that even an emotional outburst as short as the one he had with her would precipitate an angina attack, bad enough to need medication!

She was totally at a loss now. If she went against his will, it was certain to break his heart, literally. But if she denied herself the happiness she would have with Danny, it would break her heart and Danny's. "We are young enough and the wounds will heal in time," she said to herself.

The next day she met Danny at their favorite place in the College gardens.

"Danny, I just found out achan's cardiac problems are worse than I was aware. He is taking nitroglycerin pills for his angina, and did not even bother to tell me about it."

Danny was concerned, and leaning forward gently smoothed the worried frown from Radha's face, as he spoke. "Radha dear, I am sure he is in good hands with his cardiologist. If he needs better care, we can certainly take him somewhere else."

"That is not the point, Danny!" She pushed him away. I am not going to add to his problem by continuing to see you and insisting on his accepting our relationship."

"How can you give up so easily? Allow me to talk some sense into him, and he will come around."

Radha laughed in exasperation. "Danny, you know that you are not the most tactful person in this world. Any confrontation with you would only make matters worse for all of us."

"Are you saying you will not see me anymore?" His raised voice brought stares from other students walking in the park.

"Stop this, Danny. I really can't put my father's life in jeopardy for my own happiness." Radha was adamant.

"Call me when you change your mind." Danny stood up and left her sitting stunned on the cold bench.

She wept silently.

She returned to her hostel in a daze of tears. The next few days found her staring at her books, unable to grasp anything on the page in front of her. The conflict in her life was affecting her grades.

Kamala, her close friend and lab partner cornered her.

"Radha, what is the matter with you? The way you are going, you will definitely flunk your Medicine Finals next month. You had better get your act together."

Radha turned away from her.

"Come on! Talk to me, maybe I can help somehow." Kamala was not easy to get rid of.

"I am not certain Kamala, although you and I have never openly discussed this, it is no secret to you I am in love with Danny. He loves me too and has asked me to marry him."

"Then why don't you?" Kamala insisted. "A visionary such as Danny is lucky to have found a pragmatic partner in you. I am also aware you are torn between your loyalty towards your father, and your love for Danny! I really wish you would choose in Danny's favor."

"Kamala, the one thing you don't know is that my father is an ill man. His angina is affecting his work, and I hear from Ammini-Ammavi he is thinking of retiring from the bench."

"Your concern about your father's health should play a part in your decision, but don't lose Danny in the process." Kamala coaxed her. "I cannot make up your mind for you. Why don't you just postpone the decision for now, at least until your father's condition improves? Meanwhile don't say goodbye to Danny, yet!"

Heartened by Kamala's words, Radha tried to speak to her father about Danny. "Achâ! please listen to my side. I know I promised to let you arrange my marriage when I finish Medical College. Many things have happened since that were not under my control. I did not fall in love with Danny to hurt you. But, now that I have, how can I leave him? My heart and soul belong to him already."

"Oh my romantic little fool!" Judge Menon exclaimed. "You may have given your heart to him, but your life is still yours to live and your marrying him will only cause more heartaches and headaches in the future. So just end the relationship now. Your mother is weeping up in the heavens to see you arguing with me about such a serious issue. You should at least respect the fact that my age gives me a certain wisdom, and I assure you, you will suffer if you marry Danny."

"I cannot leave Danny now. Please give me another year to think about it." Her words were plaintive and painful.

"Your indecision will only give you, me and Danny more heartaches. As you have found out, mine cannot take any more pain. If you decide to continue seeing Danny, I won't be able to bear it, and you are going to be my nemesis! My doctor says I should go to U.K. for more testing. Apparently doctors there have newer tests and even new methods of increasing blood flow to the heart, and are on the verge of breakthrough with coronary bypass surgery! But I have said 'no' to my doctor. If I am in that bad a shape, I want to retire, see you get married, and enjoy the grandchildren you can give me in the late years of my life."

He took a nitroglycerin pill and placed it his mouth. Radha's face blanched with overwhelming guilt and her stomach felt all knotted inside. She was rendered speechless.

To add insult to her injury, she received notice from her Medicine professor that her poor attendance was jeopardizing her promotion to the next level of classes for coming semester.

"This is all I need. If I fail Medicine I will have to do additional rotation, and will not graduate next year with the rest of my classmates. That will definitely kill my father if nothing else does! I have to get a handle on the situation." Radha said to herself. She decided that the only thing that would save her career at that point, save her father's life and let Danny free would be to refuse to see or talk to him, anymore.

"More easily said than done." She said to Kamala, about her decision not to see Danny anymore. "The only problem is that I cannot seem to get him out of my mind. I dream of him in my sleep and even in my waking hours. I don't see a reason for living like this! Why can't I just forget about him? Why is his face haunting me so? Oh, Kamala, Please tell me what to do."

Radha was desperate. She tried to submerge herself in her books, and even managed to do extra hours of rotation in the patient floors. Danny was a special assistant to the Surgery professor, worked mainly in the operating rooms, and did not come to the patient floors, usually. This suited Radha just fine. Life was miserable enough for Radha, without having to run into Danny.

Each day she received messages from Danny in her mailbox. She had nothing new to say that would make her or him happy, and she did not have the fortitude to say the final goodbye, yet! Deep in her heart she was aware she was not being fair to him.

She still had to handle Kamala's wrath. Kamala wanted to speak to Danny and to run interference between them and Radha's achan. Radha would not hear of it.

"I need to fight my own battles, Kamala dear,." her voice curt and final. "It really has to come from my heart. If I don't have the conviction and I don't have the courage to leave Achan for Danny, then I am not worthy of Danny's affection."

"You are obstinate!" Kamala said, anger in her voice. "If you would only bury your pride and ask Danny to be patient, I am certain time will heal a lot of the rancor in your father and you will be able to go to Danny."

"Kamala, I cannot in all honesty ask Danny to place his life on hold while I work out my Karma with my Achan! If I lose Danny, I will consider it my fate to lose him and pray for his success."

"All this high-falutin' talk is not masking your pain, dear one. I know you are hurting. If you need any help from me, let me know." Kamala knew Radha well enough to know she could not do much more for Radha.

Chapter Seven

I would ask for still more-
if I had the sky with all its stars and the world with
all its riches:
but I would be content with the smallest corner of
this earth. . . if only she were mine
　　　　　Rabindranath Tagore

　　　Danny could feel the sweat pour profusely inside his surgical scrub suit, which in turn stuck uncomfortably close to his body, as he worked in theater #2. The sixteen-year-old boy under the intense lights in the operating room had collapsed on the field playing soccer and was rushed to the emergency room by his coach and parents. Thanks to an alert intern covering the Emergency Room that evening the history of a fever and abdominal pain of four days was elicited. The pain had been attributed to anxiety about a crucial soccer game and the fever was `just a mild cold', as he had put it, when his mother nagged him to get medical advice. A quick check of blood counts showed elevated white cells with a shift to the left.

　　　The two Surgical Residents on duty were already scrubbed in surgery, in theater #1, with a case of Cancer of the Colon with profuse bleeding complications. As the senior student on call in Surgical Services, Danny was next

in command to take over the care of the new case. On
further examining the patient, all the findings lead to a
conclusion of a ruptured viscus, and the young man's vital
signs were getting erratic. There was no time to waste.
Danny barked the appropriate orders of blood and other
pre-surgical preparatory orders, and started the necessary
scrubbing.

As he scrubbed for surgery he knew it would take
all his self-control to keep the turbulence in his mind from
affecting his performance in surgery. He was living in a
dreamland waiting for his Maya, Radha, to decide whether
she would marry him or not.

The last time they spoke was at least three weeks ago.
"Maya dear, the surgery professor has appointed me the lead
person among his assistants. He thinks highly of my work and
says he needs more people on his side like me." Danny was quite
elated by the news.

"Does that mean you won't be leaving town? You must
be really pleased." Radha sounded distracted.

Danny had expected Radha to jump for joy when she
learned that he was planning to stay around, and be near to her
for one more year. Her lack of enthusiasm and matter-of-fact
acceptance of the news that he would stay, dampened his spirits.

Danny and his colleague rushed the young man to
surgery. As he was being placed on the table, Danny threw
a tantrum because the blood he had ordered had not been
hung nor the drip started. "He is in a bad mood tonight,"
the lead nurse remarked to the anesthesiologist, shaking
her head. Everyone working with him knew something
was bothering him, but dared not ask him what it was.

Hurriedly, with dexterity he entered the abdominal
cavity, and found an abscess where the appendix had
ruptured, and to add to their immediate problems there
was excessive bleeding in the area, from a vessel weakened
by the inflammation. The temper, the irritability and the
restlessness in Danny were gone. His whole being was

focused on the job at hand. His amazed colleagues watched as Danny's nimble fingers quickly located the problem and without a moment's hesitation proceeded to stop the bleeding, remove the abscess tissue, and remove the culprit, in this case the young man's ruptured appendix. Periodically, Danny made eye contact with the anesthesiologist to keep track of the general condition of the patient and his vital signs. He was a master at work... a true leader orchestrating all the players in accomplishing a success story with a happy ending! He had pulled another hat-trick with the finesse of a master magician. The amazing part of it was he was only a final year medical student. Towards the end of the operation, the Senior Resident, Dr. Krishnan, having finished his earlier case in theater #1, had rushed over to help, but seeing that Danny had things under control, just stayed to watch with pride what the young genius was performing. When they were done and the abdomen was closed, Dr. Krishnan placed a firm hand on Danny's shoulder in silent congratulations. There was no need for words. The fact that Danny's "kaipunyam" saved yet another precious life on the brink of collapse was the talk of the surgical suites. Literally translated it meant that his hands had a quality akin to a Midas touch, in his case the magic of healing.

When he finished the case he was operating on he looked up and it was 2 am. It was too late to go back to the Men's hostel and he stretched himself on a cart in the students' waiting room. Half asleep, and even more dazed due to the weary body that had worked non-stop for the past eighteen hours, he was as if in a twilight zone. The visions of his youth passed in front of his eyes.

The house where he grew up was not their own.
They rented in a part of town that was near the market and
commercial area. Early in the morning, while it was still
dark outside, the rumbling of the heavy grocery trucks
delivering to the market rudely woke him up every day
except Sundays. The loud air-horns of the transport buses,
as they tried to speed up and overtake the delivery trucks,
grated on his nerves, and usually left his father in a bad
mood for the entire morning. He would go around yelling
at every one in sight. Danny dreaded facing his father on
such mornings. As a young boy Danny did not know of the
frustrations of meeting rent payments or needing money
for food and clothing for the family.

His father was a bookkeeper for one of the big textile
merchants in town. In addition he also gave private lessons
in Mathematics to children of well-to-do families for a very
nominal fee. It was common practice that the students that
needed help with the tough examinations in high school
received tutoring at home to enable them to pass the
exams. Some of the students tutored by his father went to
school with Danny. Although these children respected his
father as their tutor, they resented the discipline with
which he managed them, and more than once took it out
on Danny, picking on him during gym sessions and in the
fields. As a youngster it had bothered him. Yet, as he grew
older the resentment turned into a determination to escape
from his surroundings. That gave him the strength to
handle the tough curriculum to qualify for his Medical
School entrance exams.

To supplement their income, his Amma made
delicacies such as fancy plum cakes and steamed rice cakes
that melted in your mouth, and Danny helped her deliver
the food items in the evenings, after school. Many were the
times he caught her crying because she could not afford to
feed her own family such nice foods she slaved over the

fire cooking for other people's children. Occasionally, at the High holidays and special birthdays, she would arise extra early to cook the fancy items for her own children. The fondest memories that Danny had of growing up was the smile on her face when she set out her treats for her beloved ones instead of packing them up to be delivered to other people's homes.

He remembered how he felt guilty when his Amma had to grind the rice in the stone grinder for hours at a time. In those days there were no machines to do this and they could not afford to take the rice to mill to be ground into flour. It really did not cost a lot of money to get it ground at the mill, but they could not spare even the few paises, pennies, for such luxury. Danny would offer to help her and she usually shooed him off and told him to get back to his books. He would obey, but the noise of the grinding upset him. No, not the sound itself, but the fact that he was helpless to do anything for his mother. On occasion she would let him help, and it was then he realized how hard it was to turn the top stone on the grinder and was amazed at her strength in doing such manual labor, and still managing a graceful smile on her face.

"How can you do all this work and still be so nice to all of us? You should make me and my sister do more of these chores so you can rest or read a book once in a while," Danny would protest.

"You people have to study hard at your books, which is your main job. Don't you worry about me," she would reply with a smile.

Then he would hug her, pick up her hands roughened from scrubbing and grinding, and kiss them. "Amma, when I become a doctor, I'll make sure you have help in the kitchen and somebody to wait on you hand and foot, and you won't have to toil by the stove, and you won't even have to pick up a thing off the floor. In fact I'll make sure you are treated like a queen." She would brush off his hands, hug him close and he felt her sigh softly, and he knew she sighed both in sorrow for their present plight and in anticipation of a brighter future.

Once in a while, when his father had an especially rich client and received a windfall, they would send out the clothes to a dobie service to be washed and ironed. At those times he promised himself that when he became a doctor, he would make sure his Amma had such help all of the time.

"It is alright mon!" She would pat his head and look beyond him dreamily. "I am thankful to the Heavenly Father for giving me the strength to take care of you, my precious son. I want you to concentrate on your studies and not worry about me. When my son the doctor comes visiting, I'll make all your favorite goodies, all for you and you alone."

Danny was aware his parents had worked their fingers to the bones to enable him to complete his medical education. He owed them a great deal. Now, he was graduating from Medical School, and finally they would get a break. Although not a high salary, his Residency program would provide a big enough income for him to contribute towards some of their living expenses.

He pondered over what his relationship to Radha would do to his parents. His dad would immediately get defensive, and warn him against an alliance with a rich and powerful Judge Menon's family and advise him against jumping for the moon. His mom would want to meet Radha. She would also explain to him how Radha would have to convert to Christianity before a church wedding could take place. In her orthodox eyes where the simple faith in Christ reflected clearly, any other religion would lead away from heaven and she would not condone Danny giving up any chance of his "place in Heaven."

Growing up, his mom's blind faith would have been quite tolerable if it had not been for the fact his father constantly ridiculed her about it. Danny often wanted to yell to his father …"Stop! Leave her alone. Let her do what makes her happy!" But, he didn't. He often felt frustrated because his mom did not defend herself! As he grew older, he realized his dad's ridiculing did not dampen his mom's devotion to Christ and did not stop her frequent church-going.

Would his mom accept his marrying Radha if Radha did not convert to Christianity? It was a moot point if Radha was not going to marry him. So all he could do now was to wait and, and pray! Pray? Danny woke from his daydreams. He had not stood in front of an altar and prayed in quite a few years. An occasional "please help me God!" uttered while doing a difficult case in the operating room was the closest he had come to praying. But now with the risk of losing Radha looming in front of him his heart was trying to convince his mind that the only help he could get was from above. Then again, maybe it was too late for prayers.

Later that morning after checking out from the hospital, he returned to his room, and having bathed and freshened up, he tread the unfamiliar path to the church around the corner. The two candles in front of the altar flickered and died as the door closed behind him.

"A bad omen," he thought to himself. "Even Christ almighty is telling me it is hopeless." He walked up, relit the candles and knelt in front of the altar. He tried to focus his thoughts on praying. It had been so long! Fortunately for him, the church was empty and there were no witnesses to his misery and his agitation. He was ready to explode. He wished he could pray; he wished he could cry! No words to prayer came. No tears came either. He sat silently for what seemed to be an eternity.

When he got up and walked out of the church, he knew in his mind that he had tried to pray. He realized the issue at hand was out of his control. At that point the decision was Radha's and he simply would have to accept whatever that might be.

In the past few weeks Radha had refused to return his phone calls and would not respond to messages he left with the Medicine Department secretary. The futility of his attempts to contact her frustrated him.

In his last letter to Radha, he had pleaded with her to decide in his favor. He had also explained to her he needed an answer from her soon and had given her time until that morning, after which he had to review his options and make certain decisions about his future.

Danny then walked over to the Surgery Department offices to see what fate held for him in the way of Radha's reply.

Just as he approached the mailboxes, he was paged overhead and directed to answer a long distance call in the secretary's office.

Chapter Eight

"Do not go, my love, without asking my leave
Could I but entangle your feet with my heart and
hold them fast to my breast!
Do not go, my love, without asking my
leave... ... ."
Rabindranath Tagore

Radha walked slowly towards her favorite place in
the college grounds. The sun was hiding behind dense grey
cloud and an oppressive calm had set in. The tennis courts
were empty, except for one lone player practicing service,
all others chased away by the impending rain. The running
tracks and Cricket fields were also deserted. Even the
magenta and white bougainvillea clusters looked dull and
dreary with no sunshine to bring out their vibrant colors.

In the garden behind the College buildings, the
Cyprus trees that usually waved warm welcome to her
were ominously still, and a foreboding chill came over her.
It was not raining: yet, the air was heavy with the pre-rain
mist, and the grass felt soggy under her feet. She felt no
spring in her feet, the jasmines held no fragrance for her,
and a numbness enveloped both Nature and Radha. The
garden bench was cold, hard and un-welcoming as she sat

down to open the note she had received from Danny the previous night. She had not bothered to read it because she felt she had nothing more to say to him. But, now, a day later she felt the need to open it.

"Dearest," Danny wrote, "please give us, and our love another chance. As I have promised you, more than once, I'll plead our case with your father, personally. You cannot single-handedly shatter our dreams for our future before you let me try."

Lifting the end of her favorite sky-blue saree, she wiped her tears. She fondly remembered how Danny had bought the saree in her favorite color, for her last birthday, despite her protests. Now she wished she had enjoyed her time with him more, and protested less.

"Maya," Danny's note continued, "how can you forget all the promises we made to each other for the past three years?"

She could not complete the reading of the letter.

She rose from the cold seat, and gathering the loose end of her flowing saree over her shoulders, to cover herself against the dampness, resolutely pulled herself together in one sweeping motion. Radha walked directly to the Surgery Department Office, to find out where she could reach Danny. Danny's name was not on the Schedule-board. "Where is Dr. Daniel?" She questioned the clerk at the desk.

"Oh! Dr. Daniel has already left the department. Didn't you hear? He is leaving to take a Surgical Fellowship in Delhi." The desk clerk was surprised Radha did not know.

She fumbled out the door, her eyes misty from tears, and she reopened the letter to read the rest of it.

"Once again, Maya, I cannot live with this indecision, any longer." she continued reading. "If on Tuesday morning I don't have an answer from you, I will presume you don't want to see me again. If so, I will leave Trivandrum and you. For without you my dearest, this town holds no meaning for me. I certainly do not wish to stay and cause any pain for you. *Vidatharu, Omane',* *Vidatharu* (Goodbye, my love, goodbye)."

The tears were flowing freely now.

Radha went to the Medicine Department Office to see if she had any messages, there. She found a short note from Danny in her own slot in the mail center.

"Maya, I am heartbroken because you have not responded to my letter as of today, Tuesday, which I take as your decision not to share your life with me. I have elected to accept the Fellowship in Surgery in Delhi. It is best that we don't see each other any more. You are, and will always be, my only true love. Danny."

The final blow had fallen.

Crestfallen, Radha walked slowly through the falling rain, to her room at the Women's Hostel. Somehow she managed her way past her colleagues in the reception area and corridors and made it to her own room. Soaking wet, she was ready to collapse on her bed when there she saw the open pages of her book of poems by Tagore.

> *"Do not go my love without asking my leave.*
> *I have watched all night and now my eyes are heavy with*
> *sleep*
> *I fear lest I lose you while I am sleeping*
> *Do not go my love, without asking my leave.*
> *I start up and stretch my hands to touch you.*
> *I ask myself `is it a dream?'*
> *Could I but entangle your feet with my heart*
> *and hold them fast in my breast?*
> *Do not go, my love without asking my leave."*

Ominous words, even from Tagore. Sobbing, she fell on her bed.

Even her favorite poet offered her no solace.

Chapter Nine

It is the pang of separation that gazes in silence all night from star to star
and becomes lyric among rustling leaves in rainy darkness of July
    Rabindranath Tagore

Kamala burst into Radha's room like a whirlwind.

"Radha! It is 2 PM already, and you are still in bed?" She opened up the curtains and let in the sunlight. "You look like a ghost."

Radha woke up squinting at the sun. "Leave me and my misery alone." She protested.

"Get going girl. I came to pick you up for the party." Kamala insisted.

"What party?" Radha was confused.

"The party at the Women's Hostel in our honor. Remember we are *The Graduating Class*." Kamala shook her head in dismay. "Your achan told me that you were very upset after you spoke to Sarada, yesterday. She had no business talking to you about Danny's life in Delhi."

She sat down by Radha and spoke to her directly.

"Radha dear, life goes on. You gave up Danny over a year ago. You cannot ruin the rest of your life regretting your decision."

"Please don't preach to me. Leave me alone to wallow in my sorrow. Maybe if I drown in my tears I won't have to suffer any more."

"Oh shh...Come on now!" Kamala took stock of the disaster before her. "Your eyes are purple and large like ripe plums. Wasted tears, if you ask me. You are in no shape to go to a party tonight." Even as she spoke she lifted Radha out of her bed and pushed her to the shower and handed her the towel.

"As soon as you are dressed, we are going to the temple and then out to eat. A little prayer and a full stomach will do wonders, of that I am certain."

"How about your husband? He'll be waiting for you for dinner." Radha still stalling.

"He can fend for himself for one evening. You are my main concern right now. Let's go."

Radha knew she could not fight Kamala any more.

Kamala called the Women's Hostel and made excuses for them to skip the graduation party. Finally she got Radha out of the house, and on to the temple.

At the temple they made offerings of flowers and coconuts to Lord Ganesha.

From there they went to Xavier's Restaurant in town. By then Radha had perked up a little. Kamala asked for the private club-room upstairs. Ordering their meat cutlets with the red-onion-salad that Xavier's was famous for, they settled back to enjoy the steaming hot cups of tea served the minute they sat down.

"Do you know how many times Danny and I talked about our future in this room?" Radha spoke for the first time since they left her house.

Kamala did not answer.

Radha walked over to the window overlooking Main Rd. the central artery that ran through town.

"We sat here looking at the traffic below and longing to go out and be part of the crowds." Radha continued. "The public display of our affection would have hurt my father, and so I would not go out there with Danny. Now I have lost him forever." Her lips quivered, and her eyes filled with tears again.

Kamala placed her hand around her friend's shoulders, and spoke softly. "What is done is done, dear, and it is too late for you and Danny. You are a lovely young woman, and a darn good doctor. You have to pick up the pieces and start living again. It is no use blaming yourself, your father, or Danny for all that has happened. Now it is time to move on. You have a life ahead of you. Grab it and live it."

The food arrived. For dessert, Kamala ordered their favorite vanilla ice-cream.

Radha was still moving the food around on her plate without eating any, when the ice-cream arrived. Kamala decided that it was time to get tough. Sweet talking was not doing the trick.

"All right. If you are not going to eat your food and start coming out of this state you are in, I am going to track down Danny and will talk him into coming back here. If you really want him back, I'll do my level best to help."

Radha shot up from her chair in protest. "No...no! I know in my heart it is over. Don't even think of letting him know how miserable I am. I know I have lost our love. I do not want his pity."

For the first time since her breakup with Danny, Radha opened up to Kamala.

"Many times, Danny wanted to approach my father to explain to him how he felt. Now I feel maybe it was wrong of me to stop him. If only I had allowed them to have it out, I would not feel so guilty about ruining Danny's dreams."

Radha stopped talking. Both were silent while a waiter entered and cleared their plates.

Suddenly Radha stood up and faced Kamala.

"Can we drive back to the Medical College Campus, please?"

Kamala was surprised. "Now? Don't you think it is a little late?" She questioned Radha.

"The moon is up and I need to see our old favorite spot in the garden once more. I promise I will be all right."

Kamala instructed the chauffeur where to go, and they were both silent for the half hour drive to the College grounds, and to the garden.

The bougainvilleas had taken on eerie glows in the moonlight, the white ones with a bluish hue and the magenta ones looking dark and shiny, and not very friendly. The jasmines were in bloom.

Radha walked around and picked a handful of jasmines, and approaching their old favorite spot in the grassy lawn, spread the white flowers over it. It was a ritual of homage and goodbye to a site which had awarded her many blissful moments that she would never capture again. It was a farewell to an era in her life she would know no more.

Silently, Kamala took her hand and lead Radha back to her car. Radha's eyes were dry and her face, resolute, but now Kamala was in tears.

They never spoke about that night at the garden, nor of Danny, after that night.

Radha joined the Post-graduate program, taking up Residency Training in Medicine, at the Trivandrum Medical College Hospital.

When Kamala tried to pair up Radha with other eligible young professionals, Radha gently reminded her that `not everybody is meant to be happily married.' Kamala herself was married to a successful businessman in town and was enrolled in an OB-GYN Residency at S A T Hospital for Women and Children at Trivandrum. Being that the Hospitals were in the same campus as the Medical College itself, they met often for lunch at The Canteen, their favorite coffee shop on campus.

"Radha, I have some special news to share with you," Kamala had a sparkle in her eye and a glow on her face, as they sat at lunch, one afternoon. "I am going to have a baby!"

"Oh, Kamala, I am so happy for you!" Radha stood up and embraced her friend. She placed her palm on Kamala's tummy. "Are you still planning to finish your Residency? How are you going to manage raising the baby with the rough schedule you have ahead of you?" Radha jabbered on.

"Hold on," Kamala interrupted. I have not thought this through yet. Maybe my mother-in-law will come stay with us. If she does, I'll take three months off, and then rejoin my residency."

"I know your mother-in-law is a widow and had refused to sell her house and move in with you in the past. What makes you think that she will change her mind now?"

"She did say that in the past. But she has also said that she would reconsider, if we ever needed her." Kamala was quite confident that she would eventually complete her training.

Radha's eyes turned misty with memories of her own unrealized dreams with Danny.

Following her Residency, Radha set up practice in town. She was very successful in her private practice. She was appointed as a lecturer in Medicine at the Collegiate Hospitals, and at least in her professional life her dreams were fulfilled.

Judge Menon was very happy to have his daughter still staying at home and building up a great, thriving practice.

Naani Amma tried to talk to Radha about her pain. "I am so busy with my patients I really don't have time to dwell on the past." Radha protested, not allowing her to crack the armor.

One afternoon, Judge Raman, a close friend and colleague of Judge Menon walked into Radha's office.

"Radha-môl, you know my son Manohar? He is in town visiting me. He is a very successful officer in State Bank of India, in Bombay. I know you went to school together many years ago. I would really like it if you would get together while he is here."

Radha laughed. "You have been talking to my father behind my back. All right, I'll forgive you for that. Of course I'd like to see Manohar. It has been many years and I am sure we will enjoy seeing each other now. I just want to warn you not to raise any hope for wedding bells. I don't have any wish for a wedding at this time, and if I remember correctly, you have told me that Manohar is not one to go for an arranged marriage, either, right?"

"You are so right! I was hoping you would be able to change his mind, though!" His voice showed resignation.

Manohar was a delight to be with. For the first time since her breaking up with Danny, Radha totally relaxed with a young man of her age. Later in the evening they drove to Shankumugham beach for a stroll on the sands. They had both gone to the same grade school and high school but had lost contact once she went towards science and he to business school.

They found they had a lot in common. He too had lost his first love, not to any religious differences, but to a car accident which had left her paralyzed. He had still wanted to pursue their relationship, but the young lady refused to see him and would not even open the letters he sent her.

"That was five years ago, and I am still not ready for another relationship." Manohar explained, as they walked on the beach.

Radha spoke to him briefly about her fallout with her father about her choice in life, and admitted to him she wished things had turned out differently, however she could not open herself up to confide in him totally, and never once mentioned Danny by name.

"Radha dear," Manohar put his hand affectionately on her shoulder, "I am so sorry. We should have kept in touch in the past. Let us remedy that in the future. You know I am as close as the nearest telephone!"

Radha was thankful he did not press the issue with her. She relaxed and suggested that they go to the Mascot Hotel for dinner.

"Are you certain you feel like entertaining me?" Manohar picked up and held her hand. "I can take care of myself, you know? You really don't have to put on an act for me!"

"Of course I want to go to dinner with you tonight!" Radha insisted. She did not pull her hand away from his. "It has been a long time since I have felt at ease with any man, and you have really made it easy for me! Thank you for being so understanding."

"The feeling is mutual, Radha," Manohar said softly. "I have had my guard up with women. This is the first time in a long time I have been myself with anyone, especially if it is a woman that my father introduced me to!"

They both burst out laughing.

They dined at the restaurant at The Mascot Hotel and shared tales of horror, of trying to survive as single professionals amid well-meaning parents, relatives, and friends who were totally convinced their lives were lonely, unfulfilled, and boring without a spouse in the picture.

"Ammini-Ammavi is ready to burst into tears every time I say no to any marriage proposal, because she takes it as a sign of personal failure as my surrogate mother, that I am still unmarried."

"You should hear my mother!" Manohar was laughing so hard now, tears were rolling down his cheeks. "She not only cries about my not being married, but is miserable because she sees no heir to the fortune they are going to leave. She is upset I have not attempted to give them a grandson to inherit the family name and the family home."

"I don't think your going home without me on your arms and promising wedlock is going to help matters. You had better find a good story to distract her." Radha spoke with merriment in her voice.

"I do wish we had met under better circumstances. Maybe it would have turned out different." Manohar's voice seemed wistful.

"Maybe, but it did not happen that way." It was Radha's turn now, to talk realism. "I am still very happy we met, and I am grateful to your Dad for thinking of me."

They said their good-byes on a very cordial note, after exchanging addresses and telephone numbers, and each of them felt they had gained a long-lost sibling.

Chapter Ten

Rebelliously I put out the light in my house,
and your sky surprised me with its stars.
Rabindranath Tagore

Dr. Radha walked into the second floor Medicine ward at the University Hospital, to find it as crowded as she expected. Two long rows of beds, ten on each side, placed in military fashion, were filled with male patients, all anxiously waiting to be examined and treated. Radha's service had been on call the previous night and some of patients were very ill, demanding immediate care.

Although it was only eight in the morning, the warm summer sun shined bright through the glass windows, reflecting on the white steel bed-frames and white crumpled sheets. The starkness of the large room brought home to Radha the austerity and barrenness of the public patient ward.

She looked past the two rows of male patients and saw the two additional rows of beds for female patients in the other half of the ward, were also full. Her own small office, and an even smaller examination room, set between the male and female halves of the ward, were bare excuses for privacy between the two sections. Radha knew the patients never got used to the lack of privacy in these wards, but they seldom complained. Being in a University hospital, if the patients could not afford a private room, the wards were their only option.

"It warms my heart to see our senior medical students already hard at work." Radha smiled with pride as she greeted Dr. Alexander, her assistant and chief resident in medicine. They quickly began their rounds. The senior medical students had done the preliminary work up on many of their patients and she moved quickly from one bed to the next, receiving their reports, confirming their findings, ordering more tests and in some cases, treatments. On that particular day, the morning rounds were taking longer than usual because of the number of difficult cases.

Fortunately, Dr. Alexander was a patient young man, who kindly helped the students listen for the extra heart sound they had missed in one patient and identify an enlarged spleen in another patient whose excessive weight made it difficult to detect the spleen.

Radha had to abruptly stop listening to a patient's chest, because she heard fast footsteps and an angry voice behind her. She removed the stethoscope, and turning she saw the surgery fellow, Dr. Sivan Pillai entering the ward. He had hounded Radha all of the previous day to obtain medical clearance on a patient for surgery.

"Bed nineteen needs colon surgery. I need you to clear him right now." He was loud, impatient, and disruptive.

"Bed nineteen cannot get clearance for surgery because the ECG tracing is nowhere to be found. Please find it and bring it to me. Only then can I clear him for surgery. Even as late as yesterday his heartbeats were irregular. I'm sure you don't want to risk his going into cardiac failure on the operating table."

Dr. Pillai glared back at her, and she knew he was under as much pressure as she was. He was just anxious to get the patient to surgery. Still his attitude annoyed her, and besides his interruption had delayed her rounds.

"By the way, 'bed nineteen' as you called him, is Rama Das. Would you please refer to our patients by name, not just by bed number?" She walked away from him without waiting for a response.

Radha stopped her rounds to check her bulletin board for messages regarding any other urgent demands. A new admission was posted in her section and a red dot placed at the top right corner signaled that it was an emergency admission and took priority over the other patients in the ward that she still needed to see. But first, she had to deal with Dr. Pillai and the patient Rama Das. She turned to Dr. Alexander and asked him to please track down the ECG tracings and read them for her.

"If we don't take care of it right away," she said, "Rama Das will end up in surgery anyway. Besides, he needs his colon resection as soon as possible. Meanwhile I'll go up and see our new patient on the fourth floor."

These incidents were part of a normal day in her practice, and the hectic pace and the need for her attention to the many details kept all thoughts of her past or future pushed way back in her mind. The problems of the day required all her attention and energy. She hurried up the two flights of stairs to see her new patient.

The private floor had single rooms, but the steel beds and the stark whiteness were the same as in the wards.

Radha paused at the nurses' desk, to review the new patient's chart. She gathered that the patient was admitted an hour previously from the emergency room, where he came with a severe nosebleed. The medical student who examined him described petechiae, spotty hemorrhages on the skin of the abdomen and legs. It also said that the patient had noticed them in the past three or four days.

The chart stated that the patient's name was Prasad, 32 years old, and that he was a lawyer, practicing in town.

She walked into Prasad's room. His mother was by his bedside, her face taut and drawn with anxiety over his sudden illness. Radha said a short hello to her and kindly escorted her out of the room before she addressed the patient and his problems, which were of the utmost priority to her at the present.

Prasad looked much younger than the stated age of 32 years. He looked up at her and smiled broadly.

Despite his angelic face and his smiling eyes, she felt a foreboding that she could not comprehend. Approaching his bed, she took his right hand in hers, and introduced herself. He placed his other hand over hers, locking hers in his grip.

"Ah, Dr. Radha," he exclaimed. "I'm so lucky to have you here. I've heard so much about you, I know I'm in good hands now."

Radha laughed. "Wait a minute. I don't know what is wrong with you. Don't place so much trust in me before I figure out what you have and what I can do for you."

"At this point," he said, "I don't care what I have. In your hands even death would be *sayujyam*, salvation." Then he laughed. It was a soft rippling laugh that tugged at a corner of her heart, where not too many things had penetrated to in the past few years.

"Please, let's not talk about salvation, yet," she shook her head. When he flashed his innocent smile at her again, she felt her composure slipping. She struggled to regain her professional poise, and was serious again. "Stop laughing now so I can proceed with my examination," she pleaded.

"Okay." He threw up his hands in mock surrender. "I promise I won't complain. Even the torture of your testing I'll accept as a boon from my favorite goddess."

Ignoring his last remark, she continued with her examination. Each time she asked him to breathe; he made gasping noises and pretended to stop breathing. His tomfoolery made her laugh, but inside she was strangely stirred by this young man, who she feared was very ill.

When the first set of laboratory tests came back, she found that Prasad's white blood count was high, but she still did not know why. She ordered more tests.

Prasad prodded and nagged her for more information. "Be honest with me." He pleaded. "Am I going to die?"

"I don't have a diagnosis yet. Let's not talk about dying. Depending on what the new tests show I may have to do a bone marrow examination on you."

"What is that?" He was curious, and his voice was subdued by the fear of the unknown.

"This is a test where I will put a needle into the center of the top of your hip bone and pull out a few drops of your red marrow to see why your white cells have increased to such high levels."

"No one is going to stick any needle in my bone. No, no. The needle will break. My bones are very hard you see. Anyway, they won't find anything wrong," Prasad tried to sit up and protest. He was too frail to do so.

Radha helped him to get back on his pillow, and after she made him comfortable, she tried to reassure him, despite her own misgivings. "I know nobody likes to have a bone marrow examination, but I assure you it won't be too painful. Don't be upset Prasad, before we even do the examination. I'll talk to you as soon as I find out if you need it for sure."

More tests were done in the hematology laboratory, and Radha consulted with Dr. Theresa, the Pathologist who read Prasad's blood tests.

"Dr. Radha," the pathologist frowned. "the abnormal cells in Prasad's blood are young, immature lymphocytes, most likely indicating he has some form of leukemia."

As much as she expected the bad news, Radha did not want to hear it. She had become fond of this young man even in the very short period.

Dr. Theresa placed a hand on her shoulder. "You know that a bone marrow study is absolutely necessary to confirm the diagnosis."

Prasad's light joking manner was gone once Radha explained the need for the test. In her usual gentle manner, she described the procedure in detail. "No pain," she reassured him, "just a pulling sensation, but no pain, because I'll inject the area with a local anesthetic. We can't help you until we find out for certain what is wrong with you." She squeezed his hand.

Two hours later, she performed the bone marrow test. Prasad had grown quiet, knowing he needed to trust her decisions.

Her heart was heavy no matter how hard Dr. Radha tried to conceal her feelings, even from herself. Her foreboding came true. The tests on the bone marrow showed Prasad did indeed suffer from Acute Lymphocytic Leukemia.

Radha's next job was to tell Prasad and his mother the ominous diagnosis.

Chapter Eleven

The mystery of creation is like the darkness of the night — it is great.
Delusions of knowledge are like the fog of the morning.
          Rabindranath Tagore

In her seven years of practice in Internal Medicine, Dr. Radha had made the diagnosis of leukemia of different types, diagnosis of cancer in different sites, and of other fatal illnesses. Each time she had the onerous task of breaking such sad news to the patients and their families. On some of those occasions the bad news she rendered was mixed with good news of effective chemotherapy available at the time. Once in a while, as in cases of Hodgkin's disease, her bad news was mixed with the good news of a chance for a cure with the treatments available. Usually, her stoic personality helped her to withstand the pressure of her unpleasant task at hand, and helped her to retain a professional manner while she did so.

But this time it was different. She could not find it in her heart to face Prasad with the diagnosis of his leukemia.

"Why can't I just come out and tell him the facts like I always do?" Radha's lips quivered and she did not even try to hide her agitation from Dr. Kamala as they sat drinking tea at The Canteen, cradling a full cup of hot tea in her trembling hands.

The Canteen had always been their unofficial conference room especially on those days that they had difficult cases to handle and each needed moral support from the other. That was the place where the two met to sound off their opinions.

"I think you have already gotten too involved in Prasad's case." Kamala leaned forward to Radha, so their colleagues at the next table could not overhear. You have completely lost your objectivity. I do not understand what is going on, but I think it is my duty to advise you to watch your step." Kamala's voice was totally out of character in its seriousness.

"You of all people have been pushing me to come out of my shell for the past six years. Now I show an interest in someone, albeit a patient of mine, you are warning me? I feel different towards Prasad. I am confused, and I really do not know why. Maybe it is just empathy towards the young man and his nice mother. He is her only son."

Was she trying to convince Kamala, or was it her own self that needed convincing? Radha was not quite sure.

Kamala took her hand. "Radha, I remember when you lost a patient for the first time. I ended up staying with you to console you after you had consoled the patient's family. You were a basket case. You told me then you had been too involved with the patient's family and it hurt you too much."

"But that was along time ago..." Radha interrupted her.

"You vowed then you would never get personally involved in any of your patients' lives." Kamala continued. "You also said to me you would cry in private if you had to, but in the patient's room all they would see is 'Dr. Radha,' the consummate professional. I think I need to remind you of the promise you made."

"It is easy to be philosophical, until it hits close to home." Radha mumbled, as she remembered how she had felt a premonition when she first set eyes on Prasad. She did not know what to do about it then, and now things were less clear. She could not hand over his case to a colleague for further care. What excuse could she offer for such a transfer at this point? She was not scheduled for a vacation and she was not overloaded with cases. Even if she transferred him to another physician's care, professional courtesy, not to mention ethics, demanded she herself had to explain to Prasad the nature of his illness. After all, she had performed all the initial testing on him.

Radha had no answers, and Kamala was of no help. She shivered momentarily and she felt as if she was slipping fast down a rocky slope, and she could not stop her fall.

After leaving Kamala and The Canteen, Radha set out for a walk. The cobwebs of her past still clung to her, but she knew not how to dust them away.

All of a sudden she looked up and found herself near her personal corner of the College grounds where she used to read her poetry, before she had met Danny. She had not gone there since she broke up with Danny, and had not thought of him in a long time. Now, inexplicably, her feet had led her to the special place which had belonged to both of them. Memories flooded in. Radha was quite baffled.

Why is this happening to me now? I have a difficult case to handle and it is being made more difficult by this portentous feeling I have and by all the memories returning to haunt me. Why in the world am I so bothered by having to tell Prasad the bad news about his illness?

Radha asked the question of herself as she softly fingered the petals of the jasmines in bloom. They waved in the breeze, and engulfed her in their soothing fragrance. The ambience of the place and the favorite smells seemed to calm her mind. Her eyes fell upon a bunch of fallen jasmines, and she looked up, aware of the many that were yet unfolding. She mused; knowing that it will only last one day, the jasmine bloom still opens its widest and spreads its fragrance to the fullest, giving its ultimate gift to the world, even as it falls to the ground in its demise.

She lingered a little longer. Her breaths came more regular now, her hands more steady and her steps firmer, as she paced the floral path. She fingered her old, favorite stone seat gingerly, and sat down. It felt hard, cold, and familiar.

The honking of a car horn woke her from her reveries. Kamala had come looking for her. She was worried when she could not reach Radha in the hospital ward.

"Radha," she called out as she walked out of her car, and strode up the path to where Radha was seated. "What are you doing here in the middle of the day? In addition to your other worries, do you want a heat stroke to kill you?"

Radha arose and walked to meet Kamala, speaking as she did so. "Go back to your car, Kamala, I'll join you in a minute." She increased her pace to coax Kamala back into the car and out of the naked heat of the midday sun.

Back in the car, they were silent. The air was too heavy for words.

Arriving at the hospital, Radha turned to Kamala. "I have to be the one to give Prasad the bad news. I am also going to tell him and his Amma I will contact Dr. Bob Bell at the University of Chicago and arrange for the most modern therapy available in the world for his disease, Acute Lymphocytic Leukemia."

"Are you quite certain you want to do this yourself? You can delegate this unpleasant task to Dr. Alexander, your assistant, you know."

"No! I have to do this myself. My trip to my old sanctuary in the garden has made me realize I cannot let my past affect my clinical decisions." Radha was resolute.

"Is there anything I can do to help? Do you wish for me to come with you?" Kamala persisted.

As she walked away from Kamala and in the direction of Prasad's room, Radha turned and said to her friend, "what you can do is say a prayer for me to be strong." She saw a broad smile of relief on Kamala's face.

Chapter Twelve

No! it is not yours to open buds into blossoms.
Shake the bud, strike it; it is beyond your power to
make it blossom...
       Rabindranath Tagore

The lights were turned off in Prasad's room. Radha stepped into the darkness. A scant ray of light followed her in from the bare bulb in the corridor ceiling, and she saw that he was asleep. Two tubes, one carrying intravenous solutions and one with the infusion of blood, swung back and forth as they dropped down from bottles hung on metal poles, and shone eerily in the dim light. Radha shuddered involuntarily. She quietly retraced her steps and was about to close the door after her, when Prasad spoke.

"I am awake now. Is that you Dr. Radha? In your flowing white saree, I thought it was the silhouette of an angel. I thought maybe I had died and gone to heaven."

"Hello Prasad," Radha said, reentering the room. She flicked on the room lights. "I was leaving when I saw you were asleep. Sorry if I woke you up. I can come back later."

How I wish I could postpone this difficult task, she thought to herself. But she knew very well it was inevitable she had to face Prasad with the bad news. She also knew he had to be told soon, so that appropriate treatment could be given right away.

"Don't leave me now, doctor." Prasad's sleepy voice pleaded.

Radha pulled up a chair beside his bed and sat down.

"Prasad, I have some bad news for you." Her voice was soft, yet firm.

"I am ready for whatever you have to say." As he spoke, Prasad tried to prop himself up on a second pillow. She rose from her chair and helped him to get comfortable. As she did so, Radha saw how pale he was and how weak his arms were. She could not procrastinate telling him about his leukemia. He needed therapy immediately.

She sat down again, took his free hand in hers, and looking directly into his eyes, spoke. "Prasad, the bone marrow showed that you have Acute Lymphocytic Leukemia."

"What is that?" Prasad said as he sat up with a jerk, and the metal joints of the tubing clanged against the IV pole.

She laid a hand on his forehead and gently pushed him back against his pillows, as she spoke. "As I had mentioned to you earlier, the white cells we saw in your blood stream were very young, and that is because the lymphocytes in the bone marrow are multiplying out of control, and are coming out into the blood stream before they are mature. It is a form of cancer of the lymphocytes in your blood."

Prasad was silent.

Here I am, casually uttering words virtually destroying his hopes and his life. I don't know how to console him, and don't even know if it is my place to do so. Why am I so much more involved with Prasad's illness than I usually am with my other patients?

A sharp pain in her fingers, brought her back.

Prasad had squeezed her hand so tightly it was hurting her.

""How can I have cancer? Oh, come on Dr. Radha, I feel fine. I do not feel sick! I am strong and active as ever! Just last week I beat my brother-in law at tennis, and he is known to be a very good tennis player. I won a difficult case in court and was so excited that I could not sleep for two days in a row. How can I be suffering from, what did you say, this acute—whatever?" His voice trailed off as he bit his trembling lips.

Prasad's lower lip started to bleed. Radha grabbed a gauze pad from the bedside tray and applied pressure on the lip to stop the bleeding.

"You see Prasad, how easily you bleed? Remember the nose bleeds that brought you to the hospital? This is happening because the leukemic cells are crowding out the platelets that are needed for normal blood clotting."

"You mean to say that my silly nose-bleeds are because I have cancer? Cancer is something that happens to old people. I am not ready to die, for that matter I have just started to live. You must be pulling my leg. Dr. Radha, is this a bad joke? Is my comic brother-in-law behind this? Is he hiding outside, to come in and laugh at me when I am all wound up and upset? Oh come, come, now. Tell me you are not serious!"

His voice grew louder and its pitch rose higher, in his agitation.

Radha stood up, and said. "Prasad, I know this is a big shock to you. But you have to calm down and let me explain to you what is happening. You have to face the fact you have an illness that needs to be treated as quickly as possible. Denying the facts will not help you. Getting hysterical would only upset you and your mother and will make it harder on both of you for making the necessary decisions!"

Her firm tone and professional manner calmed him, and his breaths came easier.

"Prasad, this form of leukemia has better treatment when it occurs in young adults,' Radha continued to explain.

"So, there is some treatment." Prasad's face lit up as he spoke. "What is it? How soon can I get it?" He was ready to get out of bed.

"Wait. Wait." Radha stopped him. "In adults with this disease, the treatments have not worked well in the past; but--"

"But, what? You just said there is some sort of treatment." Prasad interrupted.

"As I was saying, recently a group of doctors at The University of Chicago had very good results with a special combination of drugs including Vincristine, and some of their patients have survived more than five years on the new regimen."

"You mean I have to go to America to get these new medicines?"

"Fortunately, I know Dr. Bob Bell at the University of Chicago. I did a fellowship there six years ago. I have taken the liberty to call him regarding your case. If you can get over there, he will start treatment right away."

She stopped talking and let the concept sink in.

"How much is all this going to cost?" Prasad said feebly.

"The treatments are quite expensive. A group of doctors here in Trivandrum are corroborating in a research project with Dr. Bell, and I can arrange for you to be included in their group of patients, so that you can get all the medicines free of charge. However, the trip itself and the stay in Chicago can be expensive."

"Then I really don't have any hope." Prasad was crestfallen, as he spoke.

"Not really so, Prasad. I have already spoken to your mother, and she says she can manage the trip, if you agree to the treatments. And, she would like to go with you."

"No. No. I can't let her do that. It will cost all her life savings. And, I would be stealing my sister's inheritance in the process. I cannot do that. What else can you do here for me?"

"The protocol of therapy available here is not approved for adults, as yet. It will be in a few years, but that would be too late for you, Prasad. You do not have the luxury of waiting."

After a few quiet moments Prasad spoke again. "When I do get these medicines you are talking about, will I lose my hair?"

"Yes." Radha knew she had to be honest.

"What happens when the treatment is over? Do I live forever? Will my hair grow back? Can I go back to work?"

He flung a whole string of questions at her.

"The treatment itself will make you very ill, because it will wipe out all the normal bone marrow cells along with the malignant cells that it is intended for. When the first course of treatment is over, special nutrients will be given for your bone marrow. Then hopefully the normal cells in the marrow will flourish and the leukemic cells will not return."

"What if I die in Chicago? Who will take care of Amma?"

"Your Amma is talking to your brother-in-law at this very moment, and they are discussing all necessary details. And, Prasad, you are not going to die from the treatments. The experienced doctors in Chicago will take good care of you."

"What do I do now? I am placing my life in your hands. Dr. Radha, do with my life as you wish." Prasad spoke with a new conviction.

From time immemorial, patients placed their lives in their doctors' hands. So, it was not an unusual request that a patient made to a physician. But, coming from this particular patient, Radha was deeply affected and she was reduced to stutters.

"I...I cannot tell you what to do." She took a deep breath. "My advice would be for you to go to Chicago. If we were to do something, anything, it would have to be very soon."

Prasad sat up and looking directly at Radha, said, "would you please ask my Amma to come in now, doctor?"

Radha nodded silently.

As she left the room to get his mother, she heard Prasad mumble "thank you." The weakness in his voice alarmed her.

Chapter Thirteen

My son, my son
He is in the pupils of my eyes, he is in my body and
in my soul
   Rabindranath Tagore

Lalitha Nair, Prasad's Amma, had not led a very religious life. She was born and raised a Hindu, and just being a Hindu, there were rituals and prayers and temple-goings that she followed like any other Hindu woman and mother. But she had not been one who found her answers in saying her prayers or in believing in God.

In the corridor outside her son's hospital room, she waited alone as Dr. Radha went in to deliver the bad news to Prasad.

———— —— ——

Lalitha remembered a vigil eighteen years in the past, when her own husband, Prasad's father, lay dying at another hospital, after he fell down the stairs in a drunken state.

Kuttappan Nair, her late husband was an alcoholic who did not hesitate to knock down anyone who stood between him and his bottle, and after many bruises and a few broken bones, sadly, she had stopped worrying about him, and concentrated on protecting her two children from the violent aftermath of his drinking sprees.

When she saw her husband unconscious on a hospital bed, fighting for his next breath, she should have prayed for him to live. She knew how miserable he himself had been in the past few years, and had not been too ardent in her wish for him to live. She did not wish him dead, but had not really care if he survived. Still, after he died, she carried an immense load of guilt for not praying hard enough for her husband to survive.

With the busy task of raising two teenagers she managed to find peace with herself, eventually. It was fortunate that his life insurance money was there for them, and it enabled them both to finish college, Prasad taking a law degree, and his sister a Masters in Special Education. Lalitha herself worked part time as a bookkeeper for a small business in town, and had managed to save a decent nest egg for emergencies.

She and her two children had led a simple life. There were no extravagant clubs or parties, and no expensive cars to drain their savings.

––––––––

Now, her only son was diagnosed with an incurable disease. How would she face her son who was dying? How do you console someone when you yourself are inconsolable?

Once again, she was waiting outside a hospital room, this time waiting for the doctor to come out of her only son's room after delivering news amounting to a death toll on his young life.

Lalitha Nair sat on the hard wooden hospital bench, and put her face down into her palms, crying softly.

An old prayer from her youth came to her lips, involuntarily.

> *"Sarwavum samarpayame!*
> *Amba nin paade!*
> *Sarwavum samarpayame!"*

I surrender all at your feet Amba (Devi), I surrender all.

The words made sense to her now. She really had no other choice than to leave it up to Amba, Goddess Mother, to help her and guide her in this time of need. Only divine help could see her through these hard times. All she could do was to surrender.

Earlier that afternoon when Dr. Radha took her into the Medicine department office and gave her the news of her son's illness, her first reaction was one of disbelief. No, it could not happen to her Prasad! "You must have the wrong blood, doctor," she had said vehemently. "How can he have a fatal illness? He is too young. See, I am still alive. How can my son die before I do? You have to repeat all those tests again. There has to be some kind of mistake."

Then she saw the look of exasperation in Dr. Radha's eyes and knew it was true. That is when the dam broke loose and her tears flowed in full force. Radha took the sobbing Lalitha into her arms, speechlessly sharing her misery for a few minutes, and the young woman's quiet strength had finally helped to control Lalitha's hysterical wailing.

As Dr. Radha held her close, she felt a warmth towards this young doctor-lady just as if she was her own daughter. Through her own tears she saw Radha's eyes were moist also. Between her sobs she heard Dr. Radha explaining there was no cure, but at a far away place in America there were some doctors who had some treatment which could be effective against the type of cancer that Prasad had. She stopped crying. She lifted her head off of Radha's shoulders and listened intently as Dr. Radha went on to tell her that it would be very expensive to get these treatments.

"How expensive?" Lalitha had asked, seeing a sliver of hope at the outer edges of the clouds of despair settled upon her.

"The treatments are very expensive." Radha had said hesitantly. "But," she quickly continued. "There are some governmental agencies and other research funds available to pay for the medicines themselves, because this is a research project. You will need to pay for the travel to the States and Prasad's stay in Chicago."

"Oh! Doctor Radha, I am not worried about the money part. I have some money saved for emergencies and I will use the very last paise of it to get any help for my Prasad. If not for my son, what is the money there for?"

"As much as I am encouraging you to get Prasad to the University of Chicago and get the treatments, I also want to warn you that there are no assurances."

"If there is no hope for cure, why should we go all the way to Chicago? What do you mean when you say they are seeing good results in some cases?"

"I mean that without the treatments Parsed will not be able to go home or function normally, but with the treatments there is a significant chance for him to get better." Radha was very persuasive.

Urging her to stay calm, Dr. Radha had gone to Prasad's room to share the bad news with him.

Lalitha remembered how, when his father died, Prasad had come to her and promised to take care of her forever. He had stayed with her and refused to get married although she could have arranged for a good many eligible girls for him to choose his wife from. He felt strongly that he had to personally take care of her, and tend to her needs. How the tables had turned on them! She had to find the strength to take care of him now. She had to nurture this sick son of hers back to health.

Her reverie was broken by Radha, whose hands felt soft on her shoulder, soft, yet strong enough to give her courage to face her misfortune.

"Amma", Radha said, it seemed so natural to address her as 'Amma' just as Prasad did, "Prasad wants to see you now."

"All right môl", she had gotten close to this young doctor, and called her 'môl', daughter, with ease. "I'll go in and talk to him now."

She got up slowly, with a concerted effort she shook off her weariness, and using her inner strength to straighten her mind and body, strode into the patient room to see her beloved son, stricken by this illness with no promises of any cure at hand.

Prasad lay still on the crumpled pillow, and in the stark white and metal background if the hospital bed, the IV poles and the blinking IV monitor, he looked lost, helpless and forlorn.

"Amma," is all he said. In his one word she heard a plea for her love and for her help.

Silently she reached down and hugged him. Her tears fell freely, and she saw that his cheeks were soaking wet. She lifted the free end of her saree and gently wiped her tears from his face.

"Don't cry Amma," he said softly but held on tight to her hand.

"Prasad, my son, what am I going to do?" She asked. "I know that I'm supposed to be strong for you. But the thought of losing you has drained me."

"You don't have to be strong for me, Amma, We will be strong for each other. There is no time for self-pity now. We have to think with cool heads and concentrate on making the right decision."

She stood up straight and faced him fully, and said. "What right decision?" The sudden strength in her voice took them both by surprise. "There is only one decision to make. I really don't mean to push you into anything you do not wish to do. But the only course of action that makes any sense, and holds any hope for us, is to go to Chicago and enter into the treatment program that Doctor Radha has advised us about. Without that hope we don't have a prayer of a future."

Prasad said, "This is the strong Amma I know and love. We still have to worry about all the money we will spend. Did you talk to my sister about this?" Prasad still had his doubts.

"I spoke to your sister about you, but not about the money. You know she will agree we have to do everything within our power to save you."

Prasad nodded.

"Your brother-in-law should be arriving here soon, and we will discuss the details later." She got up to leave. "I'll make all the arrangements through your brother-in-law. May be he would be able to accompany us both to the States."

She kissed his forehead and started to walk towards the door. She stopped, came back to his side, and taking an one rupee note (Rs.1), waved it around his head in three circles, and over his prostrate body, once, and covered his arms and legs, in an action to extract all bad vibes within him. Then she neatly folded it and put it inside her purse, separate from the rest of her money.

"I have to go and make special offerings at the Devi Temple to make your treatments a success."

She really did not have to explain her actions because Prasad knew from the past occasions that she would place that rupee note, "carrying all his bad vibes" at the feet of her deity at the temple, with a special request to get rid of them and protect him.

Lalitha saw Prasad smile at her routine of taking all his vibes to surrender them by The Goddess Devi's feet at the temple.

"That is the first smile I have seen on your face since we arrived at the hospital." She said as she walked out of the room.

Chapter Fourteen

"...I leave behind my dreams and hasten to your call"
Rabindranath Tagore...

Radha hung up the telephone. Her vacant gaze reflected her recent mood, inattentive, distracted. Her arrangements with Dr. Bob Bell at the University of Chicago had gone well, and Prasad had received his first Chemotherapy that morning. That is what his mother had called to say in that last phone call. Yet something bothered her. She could not fathom what.

She called Kamala and asked her to meet her at The Canteen.

Kamala arrived at the canteen before her. "What is on your mind?" Kamala asked as Radha sat down.

"I am not certain that I can put it into words. I feel restless. I cannot concentrate on my patients. I seem to be stuck on Prasad's problems, and I know I should not be."

"I warned you earlier not to get too involved with that patient of yours," Kamala was direct, as usual.

"I know you did. But I could not help it, and now I don't know what to do."

"Have you fallen in love with the young man Radha?"

"I don't think so..." Radha sounded tentative.

They stopped talking, as the waiter poured them more hot tea.

"I have come to see him as more than any other patient, and somehow between prescribing medications, ordering tests and consulting with his special physicians, his life had entwined with mine."

"But you don't think you are in love?" Kamala asked.

"No. I don't ..." Radha stopped, and closed her eyes for a few moments. Then she looked away from Kamala as she spoke.

"Kamala. I am considering going to Chicago to be with Prasad and his mother."

"What are you talking about?" Kamala was furious.

Radha laid a hand on Kamala's and said softly, "I know that you are worried that I am making another big mistake."

Kamala nodded.

"You know that I will never love anyone as I did Danny. I am not even sure what I feel for Prasad. But, I have this urge to be by him, and I know I will be sorry If don't."

"Can I try to talk you out of this foolishness?" Kamala was trying to help.

"I don't think so." Radha rose from her chair and left The Canteen, leaving a perplexed friend at the table.

Later she called Kamala, and told her she had arranged for coverage for her patients, and she was flying to Chicago in three days.

"So, you really did it." Kamala was still upset. "You broke your own rule and got involved in a patient's life."

"Kamala, don't be too harsh on me. You know I could not help it. I am having a hard time justifying my actions even to myself."

Kamala was quiet for a long time. When she finally spoke, her voice was soft. "Radha dear, for once you are following your heart's commands. Who am I to judge your actions? I will support your decisions and pray you make the right ones, ones that will really make you happy."

Breaking the news of her trip to her father was another matter. Judge Menon wanted to know why the trip to Chicago was so urgent. "Didn't you say that Dr. Bell would be treating Prasad? In that case why do you have to be there too?" He was not pleased.

"I want to be there for Prasad and his Amma when he receives the chemotherapy. He will be very sick after the medications. I know the Chicago area quite well and will also be able to help them get around. Especially since his Amma does not speak English at all."

"I still think you are making a big mistake. I have never heard of a doctor having to go to all ends of the earth with a patient for special treatments. But, it is your life, and you have to do what you feel is right. If you are determined to go, I hope you have a safe trip, and please call me when you get there." Judge Menon made no effort to hide his disapproval; yet, Radha saw a glimmer of hope that he recognized that she was her own person.

As the plane broke through the clouds the hazy mood of the day changed, and a blazing sun shone into the cabin. She closed her eyes shut, and the humming of the engines made her somnolent.

It was a summer evening, as she walked alone at the Trivandrum Medical College's grounds. Danny had left, to start his Surgical Residency training in Delhi. Their breakup was hard on Radha, because she knew that she was responsible for it. She walked past the floral garden, where the jasmines were still in bloom. She did not stop there, because to be alone at their special corner of the garden, where she used to meet Danny was too painful. Her eyes moist, she quickened her footsteps.

    Suddenly, dark clouds floated in, the skies turned gray, and the air was heavy with an impending rain. Amidst the darkness, a flash of light appeared in front of Radha and stopped her on her tracks. Right in the center of the glowing light, she saw the smiling face of her deceased mother. "Radha," her mother's soft voice echoed in her ears, "don't waste your time or energy thinking of what happened in the past with Danny. Do not feel guilty my sweet girl, what was done cannot be undone." Radha blinked hard to see if she was dreaming. Her mother spoke again. "Even if you are not in love with Prasad, if your heart tells you need to help him, then it is all right to go to Chicago. Don't try to fathom your heart's mysteries. Just go, trust in yourself, do what you need to do and let life happen as it is meant to be. You won't be sorry."

A flight attendant interrupted her dream. "Excuse me, we are serving dinner now; what would you like? Chicken with rice or the mixed vegetables with pasta?

    Radha smiled, relishing her mother's words. "I'll take the Chicken, please." She answered.

    Radha's thoughts took her back to of her first trip to Chicago, many years back. It had all started when Manohar, her childhood friend, came to visit with her. Manohar's friend in Chicago, Dr. Bob Bell, needed help in setting up a Cancer research program in Kerala. So, Radha pulled some strings and the University Hospital of the Trivandrum Medical College sponsored Dr. Bell for his research project. Part of his quest was to study the role of certain minerals, some possibly radioactive, in the coastal waters and sands of Kerala as a cause for leukemia in adults. The young doctor from Chicago had stayed with Radha and her father while he worked with the Cancer department at the University Hospital.

Once his data collection was done, an ongoing program of research and treatment trials between the two institutions was set up.

Two years later Radha herself won a scholarship for a year's Fellowship training in Hematology-Oncology at the University of Chicago.

It was Dr. Bell's turn to help. He arranged for her apartment, picked her up at the airport and made her comfortable in her new surroundings. She worked with him for one year and they had become close friends.

Radha mused how fate works in mysterious ways. An old friend had now come in handy to help her get Prasad the necessary care that she could not offer him in Trivandrum. And, here she was flying half way around the world to be with her patient. Or was he just a patient? If he was just a patient, why was she so nervous about this trip?

As soon as she landed at O'Hare airport, she proceeded to the hospital.

She was met at the nurse's desk by Prasad's mother. As the two ladies embraced, the younger one realized that a bond existed between them, which was more than the obvious wish on their part for wanting Prasad to beat his illness.

"Môl, daughter, I am so happy that you came. I do not have words to express my gratitude. The news of your coming has given my son more hope to go through with the treatments and has raised his spirits".

Radha took Lalitha's arm, and led her to a chair in the waiting room. She then walked towards Prasad's room.

In a small vestibule to his room, Radha donned a green gown and a mask for Prasad's protection. Prasad's white cell count was dangerously low after his chemotherapy, and without their fighting powers, any exposure to even a common cold would be disastrous.

Hence, all visitors had to wear protective garments and masks.

Her heart skipped a beat as she walked into his room. Connected in all directions to lines carrying life-sustaining blood and other fluids, lost among the white sheets and metal bars of the monstrous hospital bed, he appeared to be puppet with no control over his destiny. He looked forlorn.

Prasad turned his head as she came in and extended his free arm towards her. "Oh come quickly my darling! I have longed for this day that you would come to me ever since I first met you." Radha was taken back at his pronouncement at first. She collected herself, and walked up to his side and took the hand he extended towards her. He mustered all the strength he could and pulled her towards him. She leaned down and with great care not to disturb his IV lines, embraced him. With his free arm he clung to her as if he would never release her. After a few close moments, she gently tugged herself free, pulled up a chair and sat down by his bedside.

"Prasad," she spoke gently. Are you sure you can handle all this excitement? Maybe I came too soon."

"Oh no, no, please don't say that!" He protested. "All the pain and the nausea and the weariness of the past few days are now forgotten. You are the ray of sunshine that has chased all my clouds away!"

Then he reached over to the table and picked up a piece of paper and handed it to her. "Dr. Bell asked me to give this to you."

She opened up the folded sheet of paper and read.

Dear Radha,
As you know by now I have started Prasad on
MOP and the first course of treatment was
effective without any untoward complications.

His WBC count had fallen but is now starting to come up, but it is too slow in normalizing and hence the blood transfusion today. Sorry I could not meet you at the airport. My teaching schedule is a bit hectic right now. I'll see you later tonight at your hotel. I took the liberty of booking a table for a late dinner at the restaurant in the hotel you are staying. Will fill you in on all the details, then. If you need to reach me earlier, have the nursing staff page me, please.

Yours, Bob

She folded the letter and placed it in her purse. Lifting up her head she saw Prasad studying her face intently.

"You knew Dr. Bob well, didn't you?" his voice pique. "Will you be seeing him today?"

"Yes, later. He wants me to have dinner with him tonight". Radha saw Prasad bite his lips.

"Oh!" He was curt.

Radha laughed.

"No, don't worry Prasad, we are just good friends. Old friends that shared training and research woes for twelve months. Remember, I told you about the research he did in Kerala. Also, later on he helped me a lot when I did my fellowship here. You should be happy I have such a good friend here, when needed."

"Of course, Dr. Radha," he still spoke in a formal tone. "Of course I am pleased you are able to get me the advantages of this treatment program. I do feel stronger than a week ago, and I am even starting to eat more. Amma tells me that today I have regained the sparkle in my eyes. I told her the twinkle came from the lamp I lit especially for you today!"

Radha was aware she was not ready to face the issues that his conversation was leading up to; she sensed

Prasad had feelings for her also. She quickly glanced at her watch. "It is really getting late and I have to let you get your rest. I shall go to the hotel with Amma and your chettan (brother -in-law) and get her to get some rest too." I shall see you tomorrow. Once again she leaned down to hug him, and blinking away the tears that welled in her eyes, she turned and walked out of the room without giving him a chance to speak.

As she stopped to change from her gown and mask, she stayed a while longer to compose herself before going out to face his mother and his chettan. Seeing Prasad so wan_and weak had really affected her. She had known what to expect; in other patients she accepted the changes due to chemotherapy with a professional 'matter-of-fact' strength that was demanded of her as the caregiver. But with Prasad it was different. She felt an inexplicable ache in her chest. His eyes held a sparkle all right, but the rings around them were dark. When she held his hand, it gave away his lack of strength, despite his pronouncements of being stronger. His illness combined with the effects of chemotherapy, had taken their toll.

She vowed to herself she would try her utmost to help him through these tough days. She was glad she had acted on her whim and made the trip, half way across the world though it was. If she had dwelt on the decision much longer, logic would have prevailed, and she probably would not have come. There was no going back, now. She also realized, in her arriving by his hospital bedside, all the way across the world from Trivandrum, she had made a very personal commitment.

She walked out of Prasad's room to meet his mother and his brother-in-law.

Chapter Fifteen

"Be ready to launch forth my heart,
and let them linger who must.
For your name has been called in the morning sky.
Wait for none!"
        Rabindranath Tagore

The lights of Chicago glittered beneath them like crown jewels strewn on a black velvet cloth, as they looked down upon them from the restaurant atop the John Hancock building. Radha savored her favorite apple pie, and realized how far she was from home, because it was not a dish she would find in any restaurant back home in Trivandrum. She turned and smiled at Dr. Bob Bell, her old friend and present dinner companion.

"So how long can you stay?" Bob asked, reading her thoughts.

"I don't know, Bob." She really didn't.

"I don't mean to probe. Knowing you, I am surprised that you followed Prasad to Chicago."

"I am not sure why I came. I felt I needed to be here for him."

"Radha. . ."

She laid a hand over his, and interrupted him. "No, Bob. Don't tell me I will get hurt again. I am not the same girl you knew ten years ago." She saw the concern in his eyes. "Did you not tell me the first course of Chemo was more effective than you had hoped for? Maybe with the next one you will work a miracle."

"Let us hope so, Radha. For your sake and Prasad's."

She pushed back her chair and stood up. She did not wish to talk about it any more. "I need to go back to my hotel. It has been a very long day." As she walked towards the elevator, out of the corner of her eye she saw Bob shaking his head.

So she stayed. First, she intended to stay a week. But, after his first course of chemo, Prasad was told he had to wait for counts to stabilize before further treatments. At that point, Radha rented an apartment for herself, Prasad and his Amma, Lalitha Nair, not too far from the University of Chicago Hospitals.

While the care of his illness and his body were in the hands of Dr. Bob Bell, Prasad's heart and mind were being nurtured by Radha and Amma.

Radha called her achan to tell him her return was delayed.

"What about your other patients here? I haven't heard of any other doctor traveling half way across the earth to get his patients treatments." Her achan was pouting, Radha could tell.

"I have arranged with Dr. Kamala and another colleague to cover my practice and my teaching," she reassured her achan.

"Since I can't talk you out of it, I can just ask you to be careful, and I hope you know what you are doing."

The abrupt click of his telephone without a goodbye, spoke volumes of his disapproval.

"Déjà vu!" Radha shrugged her shoulders.

A late spring evening in Chicago found Radha and Prasad walking along the park by the lake. She had convinced him that the fresh air would do him good.

*"Lady, you have filled these exile days of mine
with sweetness,
made a foreign traveler your own."*

Out of the blue Prasad was quoting poetry.

Radha raised her brows. "I did not know you too read my poet Tagore."

"I did not before. I picked up your book of poems, and these words struck a chord with me."

"Would you like me to get you more books by Tagore from the library?"

"Here in Chicago? You can get me more of his poetry, here?" Radha laughed at his surprise.

"Yes. The rare books library is not far from this University, and they have quite a collection of Tagore, and I can even find you translations in Malayalam."

"What do you know! Yes, please. If it is not too much trouble. I would like to study the poet that you so adore."

They read more poems by Tagore during the night and walked by Lake Michigan during the day.

Radha enrolled in a short course at the Medical center in The Management of Bleeding Complications in a cancer patient. That kept her busy.

One night after his Amma had retired to her room, Radha was deep in her book, and Prasad relaxed on the couch. Looking up from her book, she saw his pensive gaze on her. When her eyes met his, he smiled; and Radha raised her eyebrows in a question.

"Oh Radha. You are a sight for sore eyes. How did I get so lucky? You know by now I am deeply in love with you. I have been since I first met you. I do not want to hurt you. So I have been fighting it."

"Prasad, the strong medicines must be playing tricks on your mind. When you feel sane again you may regret saying those words."

"If this is insanity, I'll gladly build an asylum for those who feel this way."

Radha tried to laugh away a serious pronouncement because she herself was not ready to address her own feelings on the matter.

She went back to her books. But, her reading was interrupted. Her feelings were challenged. She felt she had to respond. "I am only doing what any good doctor would do for a special patient. I just want to be supportive to you and your Amma, in this hour of need."

"Oh really!" Prasad rose and abruptly retreated to his bedroom.

Days passed with repeated testing and therapies. On a balmy evening Radha had encouraged Prasad to walk in the park by the lake. He was feeling stronger. The lake waters glimmered in setting sunlight, and a few boats lingered on the waves, despite a cold spring wind that had just picked up. As soon as she felt the chill, Radha wished him to return to the warmth of their apartment.

"Wait." Prasad took her hand and stopped her. "I cannot stand this distance any more. You are so near and yet so far away from me. I want to know why you are still staying here with my mother and me? I sure hope it is not from pity. I certainly don't want that."

"Prasad, you are right. I came to make sure you get the best care possible. And, I have been kidding myself to think that was all it was. It is time I admit to myself that I have fallen in love with you and need to be here with you."

"Does that mean you will stay here with me as long as I have to stay in Chicago?"

"I will stay as long as you need me."

Radha called Judge Menon and told him her plans.

"What about me? Who will take care of me if my heart gets in trouble?"

"I spoke to Kamala and also to Ammini Ammavi already, and I know you are all right, your blood pressure is normal and your angina is not a problem right now."

"But I worry about you. What are you getting yourself into?"

"I will take care of myself. I am a grown up now, and not your little girl. Don't worry about me any more." Radha heard a gasp at the other end, and softened her voice. "I'll always be your little girl, achan. But even you have to admit you just have to let me make my own decisions and mistakes."

"Please call me soon." At least the goodbyes were more cordial this time.

"I am sorry I have turned your life upside down," Prasad said, as she hung up.

"Don't feel guilty Prasad," she moved away from the telephone. The close quarters did not afford much privacy. "I chose to come here and be with you and your Amma. Nobody is making me do this. I will stay as long as I feel you need me. Don't worry about my achan. Ammini Ammavi and Kamala will take care of him."

"I want you to know my Amma and I appreciate your being here for us, Radha. I wish we had met under more pleasant circumstances."

Next week found them back in the hospital where the second course of chemotherapy including Methotrexate, Oncovin and Prednisone were given in high doses again. Prasad did get ill from the strong agents, but with the supportive intravenous fluids and medications to keep his nausea down, he came through without any major complications.

Dr. Bell stopped by their apartment to give them the good news that the treatments continued to be effective.

"Except that my thick head of hair is history."

Radha heard the disappointment in Prasad's voice.

"You really don't have to put up a brave front for me, Prasad," Bob was direct with Prasad, but never condescending.

As he was leaving, he turned to Radha and said. "I'll call you later with the name of the place to look for a hair-piece."

"Thank you." Prasad was quick to answer.

Radha and Prasad went to the Hair Creations store the next day. Prasad had a hard time with choosing any. The dark ones looked "too fake," as he put it, and the brown ones made him laugh when they placed them on his head.

"I am not going to Trivandrum with a bald head." He was sulking.

After umpteen tries, he finally found one that he liked.

As soon as his white blood counts returned close to normal, Dr. Bell gave them clearance to return to Trivandrum. Through the entire return flight, Prasad was preoccupied with his hairpiece.

Prasad's sister met him at the airport as they exited the Customs clearing area. She reached up and grabbed his face in both her hands and said. "I thank Lord Krishna for bringing you back to us." Then she stepped back a few paces and looked him over. "Not bad. Not bad at all." She continued. "I thought you would be so weak that we would have to carry you home on a stretcher. Not as good-looking as I am, but you look pretty good."

Prasad winked at Radha and mumbled, "I don't think she recognized that I am wearing a hair-piece, right?" He was thrilled that their secret had not been exposed.

Soon they were walking out of the airport, Prasad happily recounting to his sister, all the details of his stay in Chicago, about the town and the people. When he described the rigors of his chemotherapy, he sounded like a victorious war hero.

Chapter Sixteen

No mystery beyond the present; no striving for the
impossible;
no shadow behind the charm; no groping in the
depth of the dark.
This love between you and me is simple as a song
        Rabindranath Tagore

It was Dr. Radha's first day back at her clinic in
Trivandrum. The elderly patient, Pankajam, a woman 72
years old, was having great trouble breathing and could
hardly answer Radha's questions because it took all of her
energy to breathe.

"Pankajam, did Dr. Soman Nair see you last month
while I was gone?" Radha asked.

"Yes doctor, he did. He suggested some tests and
also gave me a new prescription." Pankajam smiled
sheepishly.

"So? What happened when you took the new
medicine? Did that help?" Radha was puzzled.

"I did not buy the new medicine. Of course I was not
going to change the medicines you gave me without your
permission." Pankajam was indignant.

Then, between gasps she whispered. "I don't trust
anyone else."

Radha smiled and shook her head. "But, Pankajam, you are in heart failure now. I have to admit you in the hospital and change your medicines.

"All right doctor." Pankajam sighed with relief. She was breathing easier already, now that Radha was in charge.

That was just one example of almost a dozen of Radha's patients who had waited for her return to get proper care.

Her patient visits were further interrupted by requests for review of orders by other nurses, or for her signature on various papers by administrative personnel.

"What a week!" She commented as Radha met up with Kamala at the end of the first week back.

"You do look tired Radha. But that is what you get for making yourself indispensable to half the world." Kamala laughed, as she chided Radha. "But, your cheeks are flushed and your eyes sparkle despite your exhaustion. What is going on?"

"Kamala, I am happy and excited. Prasad and I have talked. You were right when you told me you thought that I was in love."

"I am glad you have finally admitted that." Kamala smiled as she hugged Radha.

It was a different scene at her father's house. When Radha introduced Prasad and his Amma, Lalitha, to Judge Menon, he turned to Radha with raised eyebrows loaded with the question, "what now?" Then his civil nature set in, and turning to Lalitha, he cupped his palms together saying, "Namaste," invited her into the house, made her comfortable in the drawing room, and inquired politely about her stay in Chicago. "Radha had asked me to go visit her while she lived in Chicago, but I have no interest in traveling that far. And of course my practice demands my presence here in town."

Radha and Prasad exchanged smiles at the jab Judge Menon made regarding Radha leaving her practice to go off to Chicago for Prasad. The sarcasm was not lost on them.

Prasad and Lalitha stayed for dinner, and Radha sighed in relief when they left.

It came as a pleasant surprise that her achan took a liking to Lalitha, and made friends with her quickly. Many times a week the four of them met for dinner and occasionally Ammini Ammavi joined them. The three older members spent most of their time reminiscing their youth.

Two months later the third course of Chemotherapy was given at the University Hospital in Trivandrum, under the care of Dr. Mary Chacko. She was a Hematologist-Oncologist who had been trained at the University of Chicago, and was now collaborating in the Research and treatment protocol set up by Dr. Bob Bell.

One evening after dinner Judge Menon and Lalitha went to visit mutual friends, leaving the two younger people to an evening of privacy. Radha and Prasad both enjoyed listening to light classical music and as the melody of P._Leela played in the background, Radha sat at her desk with her Medical journals she had missed while she was away, all in chronological order, with the oldest one open in front of her. Prasad was comfortably ensconced in the soft, wide couch, wearing new sweat pants that he had bought in Chicago, and also had a law book open on his lap.

It seems like some color has returned to his cheeks, Radha thought as she watched him from the corner of her eye. "I hope to God that the remission stays prolonged, and maybe he will return to his firm one of these days," she muttered; more of a prayer than a declaration.

Her mind wandered back to when her Amma was ill, and remembered how she was too young to know what was happening. It was much later she had found out exactly how her Amma had died. At least now she was well apprised of Prasad's condition, and was even able to contribute to his care. Lost in thought, she had imperceptibly let her book fall to the floor.

She looked up and saw Prasad standing beside her. His arms were crossed across his chest, the expression on his face was soft and pensive and his eyes were misty. She jumped up from her chair, a frown clouding her eyes.

"Oh no! I did not mean to startle you. Don't worry, dear. I'm alright." He appeased her fears. "I was just thinking that our paths have crossed and merged for a very good reason. I have found a guardian angel in you. But, it makes me wonder, what do you get out of this?"

"Prasad!" Radha's voice held a tinge of indignant impatience, "do you think for a moment I would have stuck around this long if I was not getting anything out of this? You know I care about you deeply." Thus speaking she got up from her desk, and moved over to the sofa.

Prasad sat down by her on the sofa and took her hand in his. "Radha dear, I know not how long, or what kind of life, I can offer you. But, I want to share it with you, for the rest of the time I have in this world. I want to share with you the best of what is left in me. Will you marry me? I know that it may not be a *'long happy married life'*. But, I promise to make you happy as long as I live. I know I am being extremely selfish. Forgive me..." Sobs interrupted the flow of his words.

Radha moved closer to him. She saw he was shivering, from the effort of his long speech as well as from the emotions that had flooded up so quickly. She hugged him and held him close until he stopped shivering.

She lifted his head gently with both her hands, and looking directly into his dark brown eyes, she spoke. "Yes, Prasad, I shall marry you."

Prasad sat up with a start. He was stunned at her quick response. "You really mean what you just said, don't you?" He ran his hands through his hair, as if to clear his thoughts. Then he moved closer to her and said, "but...wait Radha, I know I'm madly in love with you. Blinded by love for you, I may not know what I am doing to you. But you should see clearly for the both of us, and if we are making a mistake, let us stop right now. What can you see in me now?"

Was he trying to dissuade her? Radha was convinced he had expected her to say 'yes.' She placed a finger on his lips silencing him. "Prasad, I love and care about you. I will be very happy to be your wife." They held each other wordlessly for the longest time. Finally Radha got up from the sofa.

"It has been a long evening. I want you to go home now, and get some rest. Tomorrow we shall talk to your Amma and my achan and make plans for our wedding." Radha's voice was gentle.

Early next morning, Radha went the Krishna temple for special blessings before she broke the news to her achan. She took a bath and changed into a classical two-piece sari outfit, called a *mundu & neriyathu*, unique to the people of Kerala, made from non-bleached cotton with gold-dipped threads woven into a design at all borders, and worn draped over a short choli-blouse. Seeing her reflection in the hall mirror, she remembered her own Amma as she used to wear the very same outfit on her trips to the temple. Radha's eyes grew moist.

At the temple, Radha placed an offering of fresh flowers, roses and chrysanthemums, at Lord Krishna's feet, and stood still with her eyes half closed and hands cupped together in front of her in prayer. After chanting her usual prayers, she voiced her wishes to Lord Krishna, fully expecting him to hear them. "*Oh Lord, please give me the*

strength to stand up to my achan, and to convince him that I am
doing the right thing for me."

Returning home, she placed the *prasadam* from the temple, which included the sandalwood paste and the flowers that had adorned the idol of lord Krishna for the morning pooja services, in front of her Amma's picture. She lit a lamp in Amma's honor. Then she joined her achan at the breakfast table.

"I have something to tell you. Prasad has asked me to marry him and I have told him, yes." She did not see any point in beating around the bush.

Judge Menon's hand stopped, the spoon with his food was suspended in midair, while he stared at Radha's face in surprise. Then slowly he put the food back on his plate, gulped hard and spoke. "Did I hear you correctly? Did you say that you accepted his proposal without even discussing it with your own achan?" His voice rose a syllable with each sentence. "And you ask me to trust your decisions as an adult? How can I treat you as a responsible adult when you go make decisions that are obviously to your detriment? How can you expect me to sit back and approve of your actions when I know as well as you do about Prasad suffering from leukemia, which makes his future uncertain, to say the least?"

"Achan, please don't get so upset. As you have just revealed by your remarks, I was right in accepting Prasad's proposal before consulting with you. I was quite certain you would not approve of it. But, you really are not being given a chance to oppose me in this. As much as I adore you, I have to live my life as I see fit and I have made my decision. Right now Prasad's disease is in remission, and I am willing to take a chance on a future with him."

"Please think about it for a few days before you jump into this blindly." Judge Menon made a weak attempt, once again.

"No use in stalling, achan, I am not going to change my mind. We will share the news with Prasad's Amma and with Ammini Ammavi today. I will leave it to you and Ammini Ammavi to come up with an auspicious date and time for our wedding as soon as possible." Radha got up from the breakfast table and went around and hugged him.

"It will really mean a lot to me, to us, if we can do this with your blessing."

Judge Menon held her tight. "I almost lost you once. I do not want to take that chance again. Yes. You are an adult, a practicing physician, and I have to believe you know what you are getting into. I know when I am defeated. I might as well help you with your plans." He grumbled, as both of them left the table, leaving two plates filled with food, untouched, uneaten.

It was different with Ammini Ammavi. When she heard of Radha's plans she burst into tears. She refused to believe it. She paced the floor, wringing her hands and shaking her head.

"Ammini Ammavi, dear, please believe me when I say I love Prasad, and I really want to marry him, settle down with him and be a friend and wife to him."

"How can you settle for a life with an invalid with no hope for a future?" Ammimi Ammavi asked Radha.

"I can lead a normal life with him," Radha said, as she took both of Ammini Ammavi's hands in her own and made her sit down. Radha had to repeat all her reasons over again.

"You know, after the wedding we will stay at my achan's house?" She continued. "Remember, if I got married to somebody from Cochin or Kollam I would be moving away from all of you. Now you don't have to worry about that."

Radha's frail attempt at humor fell on deaf ears.

"How can you joke about this? Your Amma is not here and it is my duty to remind you that you are the Lekshmi of this house?"

Radha could not help laughing at her being compared to the goddess of wealth and prosperity.

Ammini Ammavi pushed Radha away from her, stood up to face Radha and spoke sternly. "Don't forget you are our hope for the future of this family and that you have a responsibility to have children and to keep our future generations going?"

"Ammini Ammavi, don't you think my happiness in this life is more important than the issue of any future offspring?"

Ammini Ammavi just burst into tears.

After a few such arguments, Radha refused to talk to her Ammavi about Prasad, or her wedding plans.

She was seated in her favorite seat in the garden at the Medical Campus, and she held Tagore's book of poetry in her hands. Danny came up behind her and demanded: "give me that book, Radha. You have no use for poetry in your life, now that you have given me up for good." She stood up and hesitantly handed him the book, the very book that held words that sustained her through many a crisis. The whole world went dark. She could not see. Neither the trees that she knew were around, nor the hands of Danny that took her book from her just a second ago were visible. She screamed.

Radha woke up in a sweat. What was going on? Was it an omen? She looked around. The afternoon sun streamed in through the windows of her living room. The medical journal that she was perusing, lay open in her lap. She must have dozed off.

She called Kamala.

"How could I have said yes to Prasad, knowing that a part of me still belongs to Danny and will always remain that way?" Radha asked Kamala, after she had described her dream. "What if I am doing Prasad a disservice in marrying him?"

"You have been honest with Prasad, and now it is time to be honest with yourself." Kamala leaned over and took Radha's hand.

They were at the Canteen and Radha's tea was getting cold.

"I have not seen or spoken to Danny in twelve years. Why am I having these dreams now?" Radha asked Kamala.

"It does not really matter, Radha. If it is Prasad you want to find happiness with, I think you should go for it," Kamala was quite convincing.

"Thank you for being so patient with me and putting up with my moods." Radha replied, relief in her voice.

Prasad's Amma was happy. She had made no secret of how she felt about Radha, and was thrilled to welcome her as her daughter-in-law.

Later that year Radha and Prasad were married. In a quiet ceremony, attended by immediate family and a few close friends, they tied the knot at a temple in Trivandrum. Radha being the daughter of a prominent Judge, and a popular physician on her own right, their wedding would have been an `event of the year' occasion, under different circumstances. But not this time. There was no formal dinner for a thousand people following the wedding. There was no throne-shaped sofa on which they would have been ceremoniously seated and be exhibited to the entire world as the `newly-weds' in a post-wedding reception.

As is usual for a Kerala wedding, a Kathirmandapam, gazebo of flowers, was set up in the temple grounds. Strands of jasmines, oleanders and chrysanthemums hung from all sides of the gazebo, and in the center, a wooden seat covered by a cotton cloth with woven golden borders was placed where the bride and groom would be seated for the ceremony. To one side a large brass oil lamp held seven glowing wicks, which shone brightly on a big mound of rice grain, a sheaf of rice stalk, and a head of pale yellow flowers from the coconut palm, all signs of prosperity and good luck. Incense burned profusely, enveloping all present with a smoky surrealism.

At the beginning of the ceremony, seven young girls dressed in colorful silk finery and carrying shiny brass trays filled with flowers and a small lamp in the center of each, walked in slow procession to escort the bridegroom to his seat in the gazebo. As he waited, the same girls went back to the bride's dressing room to escort Radha to the gazebo, for the wedding ceremony.

Radha had selected a red and gold brocade sari with a matching gold blouse for her wedding ensemble. "You make a gorgeous bride." Ammini Ammavi spoke with love, as she wove Radha's hair into one long braid down her back, in traditional fashion. Then she adorned the braid with garlands of jasmines, giving it a special lift, and enveloping Radha in a mist of heady fragrance. "I wish your Amma was here to see you."

"You have been my 'Amma' for most of my life, Ammini Ammavi, and you are here with me. That is what matters today. I am grateful for your blessings. I do feel beautiful. Thank you." She hugged her Ammavi.

Now Radha herself was being escorted to the seat in the gazebo for the nuptials with Prasad. As she approached the gazebo, the scent of the thousands of jasmine and chrysanthemum blossoms wafted her back to the Medical college grounds where the fragrance of the jasmines linked her to Danny, a lifetime ago. Her steps faltered, but only for a moment. Ahead, Prasad's face smiled up at her. Lit by the soft glow of the brass lamp, the hope and anticipation she saw in his face gave her the momentum to complete her steps to reach his side by the gazebo.

Prasad's dark hair was combed back, and he wore a simple white cotton shirt and white cotton mundu, draped like a sarong, as was customary for a Kerala bridegroom. There was no sign of the rigors of his disease or the therapy on his face. Instead his cheeks were flushed, partly from the excitement and partly from the reflection from the red roses in the garland of welcome that was placed on his neck, earlier.

Amidst chanting of prayers in Sanskrit by the priest, the beat of drums, music of classic saxophones and the melodious but loud ringing of temple bells, Radha and Prasad exchanged floral garlands and signet rings to tie their lives together. The usual pomp of a thousand guests was not missed by either, as they were surrounded by the few close friends and family, who hugged them close in hearty congratulations.

They decided not go away on a honeymoon, since both their jobs demanded their immediate presence.

"You really don't mind us staying in my father's house, do you?" Radha asked Prasad when the many boxes containing his books and all the suitcases with his clothes arrived the next day.

He gathered her tight in his arms and said. "Your achan has tried hard to be gracious about our marriage. The least I could do is not to take you away right now."

"Besides," he added with a twinkle in his eye, "it is so convenient to live close to town, rather than commute the hour each way from my Amma's house."

Radha laughed. She reminded herself that his sense of humor was one of the reasons that attracted him to her in the first place.

"Whatever your reason, Prasad," she said cuddling close to him, "I am quite happy I do not have to upset my achan and his ailing heart by moving away with you at this time."

Chapter Seventeen

We laugh at solemn death till he joins in our laughter,
We tear open Time's purse, taking back his plunder from him.
            Rabindranath Tagore

The morning sun streamed into her kitchen, as Radha warmed up the griddle to make dosas, Indian pancakes made without eggs, for breakfast. To make the special batter for the dosas, lentils from a black bean called urad dhal, and rice grain were soaked for four to six hours, then ground for an hour until a very thick batter was made. This batter was on the counter-top, at room temperature, overnight. The batter had risen to fill a six-quart, round, steel bowl. A smile lit up her face. She was pleased, because, the higher the batter raises, the softer the dosas. Though not a very good cook, that much she knew.

She chanted along as the *Suprabhatam*, the daily morning wake-up prayer for The Lord came on the radio, punctually at seven o'clock.

Until her marriage to Prasad one year ago, Radha did not have the responsibility of cooking for anyone, and Madhavi, the cook and housekeeper in her achan's home did all such chores. After their wedding, Radha and Prasad had moved in with her father, and Radha started taking more interest in preparing their meals. The dosa batter had been one frustrating challenge to master.

She mixed salt into the dosa batter and checked the griddle with a drop of water. She jumped back as the water sizzled to let her know the griddle was ready. She ladled the batter on to the warm griddle and turned down the flame of the burner, so that the dosa would cook evenly. Many times in the recent past, her dosa burnt at the edges before the center was quite done because she set the burner too high. This morning she was determined to make perfect dosas for Prasad, her achan, and for herself.

She took the Sambar, a spicy mixed vegetable curry that was used as gravy to dip the Dosa in, from the refrigerator, and placed some in a pot on the burner next to the griddle, and started the burner.

The Suprabhatam chanting ended, indicating that twenty minutes had passed by. By then she had cooked enough dosas which now filled the oval platter that she had placed close to the stove-top to keep them warm. She turned around and stirred the simmering Sambar. The strong smells of asafetida and the tamarind in the Sambar filled the room with a mouthwatering aroma. She turned off the burners.

Radha washed her hands, and went to the bottom of the stairs. "Come on down Prasad and please make sure achan comes down with you. Dosas and Sambar are ready and waiting."

She poured herself a cup of coffee from the thermal carafe Madhavi had placed on the table, sat down on one of the comfortable, cushioned chairs, and opened the morning paper as she waited.

Soon Prasad and Judge Menon joined her, and breakfast was served.

"I see married life suits you so well." Radha's achan remarked as he finished his breakfast, rose from the table, and walked over to Radha's chair to kiss her goodbye, before he left for Court.

"Yes achan, and I am glad you noticed." Radha laughed.

"Are you going to be late tonight?" Judge Menon continued to talk while he tied the knot on his tie, and picked up his leather portfolio on his way out.

"No. But I am going to meet Prasad at the Courthouse and we will stop by Kamala's house for a visit before coming home. We have both been so busy we have not seen Kamala and Biju for the last few days. Kamala called last night to complain."

"As if she needed an excuse to see Kamala?" Prasad teased as he too got up from his chair and picked up his papers off the hall-tree, and donned his robes for the Court.

"Well, I really do want to see Kamala tonight. You don't mind do you?" She walked to Prasad and hugged him. "'Bye dear and see you later," she said and she walked up the stairs to get ready for the hospital, as the men walked out the door, which was opened for them by their chauffeur, Kumara Pillai, who had already pulled the car out to the front of the house.

Radha was dressed and ready to go to the hospital by the time the chauffeur returned from taking Judge Menon to his chambers and Prasad to his firm. Kumara Pillai, who had driven their car for more years than Radha could remember, was not just a chauffeur. He was a friend.

"Prasad looks good, Radha-môl. Is he cured of his disease?" He addressed her as môl, daughter, and treated her like his own.

"I can't tell if he is cured, Kumara Pillai. But, I do know he is in remission, which means he does not have the disease right now. I am hoping it will remain that way for a long time."

"It is so good to see you laugh more nowadays. This is good. You know we all want you to be happy." Kumara Pillai said, as he closed the car door for her. "I pray to Lord Krishna for you and Prasad, every day," he continued.

"Thank you," was all she could say, she was touched by his show of affection.

Later the same evening, Radha walked into the living room to find Prasad comfortably ensconced in the sofa reading his case files. She smiled to see how the room had not changed since her high school days, when she had made herself comfortable in the same sofa, cuddled among the same, plush, green velvet cushions, while she prepared for her chemistry exams. A cloud of sadness settled on her face when she remembered how the sofa and the cushions had welcomed her on sleepless nights when she pined over Danny, and she was certain the stains from her tears would still be visible, if she cared to look for them. She shook her head, as if to shake off the memories. That was in a different lifetime.

She stepped forward, and bent down and kissed Prasad. He looked up, and she saw a frown on his face.

"What is troubling you Prasad?" She asked softly.

Prasad was silent.

Radha sat down by him awaiting an answer.

Minutes later he spoke.

"I hate to bring this up, Radha dear," he paused. "Next week it will be one year after my last chemotherapy. Are we supposed to go to the University of Chicago for a checkup?"

"You know, Prasad, I had just received a note from Dr. Bob Bell a couple of days ago, and was in the process of checking our schedules to see how soon we can go over there."

"I can free up my schedule without too much hassle. All my cases are familiar to my partners and they can take over any time." Prasad was anxious to find out how well his remission was lasting.

Honoring the eleven-hour time difference between Trivandrum and Chicago, Radha called Dr. Bell later that night, when it was morning in Chicago, and she located him at the hospital.

After the initial greetings, Radha got to the point quickly. "How soon do you feel Prasad has to come over for his follow up?" She asked.

"As soon as you can." Bob was his usual cheery self. "I am really pleased that you can come over to Chicago this time. There are some new Genetic studies available that we can do on Prasad's bone marrow cells. It would guide us better in his treatments, just in case he gets in trouble later."

"Do you think he might be in trouble now?"

"Oh no." Bob was quick to allay her worries. "The new tests will give us more insight if Prasad ever needs a bone marrow transplant."

Radha had nothing to say.

"Don't worry Radha." Bob reassured her. "Just come as soon as you can. I'll set up an appointment for two weeks from now, and you let me know if you can make it."

She agreed.

Radha and Prasad flew out to the University of Chicago by the end of the same week.

For the next few days they poked and probed and took pictures of Prasad's entire body. Many a time he protested, saying how he felt perfectly normal and did not want any more blood drawn for testing. But each day Dr. Bell came up with one more reason for additional tests to be done.

"Please Radha, let's go home!" He said to Radha when one more new test was ordered.

"You can't leave now." Radha replied, placing ice packs on his forehead to relieve a bad headache that he was experiencing. We can go home only after Dr. Bell gives us the good news you are still in remission."

The next week of waiting was pure torture, while they waited for the verdict. Finally Dr. Bell's office nurse called to say he was ready to see them. They rushed over to his office.

Dr. Bell greeted Radha with a hug. Smiling broadly, he turned to Prasad. "I have good news for you. Great news, actually! The leukemia is still in total remission. The bone marrow shows a good healthy population of normal cells and your system shows no evidence of any infections, Prasad. The blood counts are holding up, and I feel we've won the battle."

"Did you hear that, Radha?" Prasad sounded like a little kid who was just been given cotton candy. "Let us go celebrate." He grabbed Radha by her arm, and was almost out the door. Then he stopped, turned around and took both of Dr. Bell's hands in his and shook them. "Thank you." And before Radha could even say a word, he had her out the door.

He flagged down a taxi and asked to be taken to the Buckingham fountain. All the way, he held on tightly to her hand. He talked incessantly of how he was going to see all the sights in Chicago that she had told him about. "Didn't you tell me that you came here to relax when you were here for your training?" he asked Radha as they alighted from the cab.

"Yes, Prasad. This was one of my favorite places when I lived here."

The fancy shaped animals that spouted water on all sides of the elaborate fountain fascinated Prasad. The sounds of water soothed them as they sat side by side on a bench, eating ice-cream cones, and looking upon the myriad colors of roses in the adjacent Rose Garden. At night-time, the dancing waters of the fountain were made even more magical, illuminated by the white, red and blue lights, flashing in alternation with the shorter periods of yellow, orange and green.

They returned to their hotel, late, tired and happy. As Radha opened her purse for the hotel room keys, she was surprised to see a pretty blue box with silver bow on top in there. She looked up to see the flicker of a suppressed smile on Prasad's lips, as he faked surprise.

As soon as they were inside their room, she opened the box. Staring up at her was a single marquis diamond, dazzling her eyes and warming her heart. Turning to him, tears flowing down her cheeks, she hugged him tight.

"Radha, don't cry. You are the sole reason I am alive today. Not only free of my disease, you have lit up my heart with the hope of life. I want you to remember this whenever you set eyes upon this little sparkler." He led her to their bed, sat her down and slipped the ring on to her empty left ring finger. In the true Nair tradition of South India, her wedding band had been a gold signet ring that was placed on the right ring finger at the time of their wedding. "I also want this western token on your left ring finger to remind us of the part that this great city of Chicago has played in enabling us to go on with our lives. For that, I am ever thankful."

"But, when? How did you manage this?" Radha looked from Prasad to the ring and back. "Who took you shopping?"

"Oh! While you went to visit your friends at the University last morning, Bob took me to C.D.Peacock's. Now, that is some store. You should go there sometime." He came around the bed and sat by her. "I wanted to surprise you." He whispered in her ear.

"That you certainly did." She nestled her head on his shoulder. "You know I don't need any shining baubles to know how you feel about me. Yet, I'm really happy you are well enough to go shopping for me."

The next day they decided to take in some old classic movies at the Museum of Broadcast Communications. They both cried with Scarlet when Bonnie died in Gone with the Wind, and sang and laughed with Doris Day in Pillow Talk.

That evening they were guests at Dr. Bell's house for dinner. Bob was still a bachelor, and they met his lady friend, Janice who efficiently kept the conversation at the dinner table away from medicine, treatments, statistics of survivals after treatments, and any such topics which would even remind them of the nature of the primary reason for their trip.

Janice was a legal secretary at a large law firm in Chicago. Janice had gotten them seats in one of the skyboxes that her firm owned for a Chicago Cubs baseball game, and being guests of Janice and Bob, they were given royal treatment with drinks and hors d'oeuvres served by uniformed waiters and waitresses. At the break at 6th inning, dinner was served. It was quite elaborate with barbecued chicken and three different kinds of salads, and also included hot dogs and hamburgers for those who wished a simpler fare. Everyone left happy because the Cubs beat the LA Dodgers in the game.

"I knew that we Indians were crazy over our Cricket games. I am surprised these people could beat us in their enthusiasm." Prasad remarked as they got ready for bed that night.

"Baseball. Not Cricket, Prasad." Radha corrected him.

"It's all the same." He did not want to be corrected, and Radha just laughed.

With the realization they were given a second chance for happiness, they decided to make the best of it. They cherished the moments together, and often Radha read out loud from her books by Tagore.

"I thought that my voyage had come to its end
at the last limit of my power,
- that the path before me was closed,
that provisions were exhausted
and the time came to take shelter in silent obscurity.
But I find that thy will knows no end in me.
And when old words die out on the tongue,
new melodies break forth from the heart;
and where the old tracks are lost,
new country is revealed with its wonders."

And new countries they did explore. For the first time since they were together, they lay side by side and explored the curves and corners of each other's bodies, barring all inhibition; now they knew he was really healthy. Thoughtful, caring and kind, they were yet bold enough to bring each other's deeper-most pleasures to the surface until they found total contentment in each other.

They explored their minds and their souls as well, questioning each other's beliefs and friendships. They asked questions of their friends that they would not and could not ask in the past, because of the precarious nature of Prasad's health. They could not rock the boat in the past. Now that their boat was sailing strong and stable, they were ready to tread stormy waters, if needed.

One of their most memorable visits was their sojourn to the Art Institute of Chicago. Studying the century old impressionistic paintings of Monet and Manet, and the real life expressions of Gauguin, they commented on how eternal life is and how fortunate they were to share this small fragment of eternity together. The immortality of the scenes in those paintings heartened them both.

In front of Monet's painting of 'Rough Seas at Etretet,' Radha's face fell and she was silent. "Are you thinking of your time by the sea in a different beach, Radha?" Pointed and direct, Prasad's voice was still soft and without rancor.

"Yes." She turned around and faced him as she spoke.

"Talk to me dear. I see it still hurts you to think about it." Prasad was persistent.

"How much of my story do you know? What do you want me to say?" Radha asked hesitantly.

Prasad placed his hand around her shoulder and veered her out of the Impressionist hall, found their way to the Garden restaurant, and on to a quiet corner table.

"Many a time I see a shadow of your pain lurking in your eyes, behind your laughter and even behind the twinkle of happiness, of which I hope I am the cause."

"I really have gone past the pain, Prasad." Radha tried to convince him. Radha knew that Danny's name, although never spoken aloud, still hung in the air between them. Both knew whence the pain in Radha's eyes came from, even if Radha refused to acknowledge it.

"Are you certain my love? Is there anything I can do to help?"

"You have already helped. In your love I have found my happiness and I truly love you. I have really left my painful past behind."

Prasad took both her hands in his, and they sat silently gazing into each other's eyes for a while. When both realized that nothing more would be said, they rose, and returned to their hotel room.

Visiting the Egyptian exhibit at the Field Museum of Natural History, they laughed at the Mummies and decided they would not want to be preserved like them anyway. The exhibit of the Neanderthal man reminded them that the use of words to express their feelings, was definitely an improvement over their predecessors. They were like kids again. They forgot their worries about her past and their future and lost themselves in the novelty of experiencing such wonders together for the first time.

Chapter Eighteen

A drop of tear,
Glistening white on the cheek of eternal Time-
this Taj Mahal.
      Rabindranath Tagore

After the few fun-filled days in Chicago, Radha and Prasad returned to Trivandrum, back to their loved ones.

Their chauffer, Kumara Pillai met them at the airport.

"Where is my Amma? How come she did not come to meet us? And what happened to Radha's achan? He didn't come either?" Prasad did not hide his disappointment, as he grilled Kumara Pillai with his queries. "Are our parents too busy to come with you?" He continued without giving Kumara Pillai a chance to answer. "I just thought they would be anxious to see me after they received the good news of my normal tests."

"Of course they are anxious to see you. They are waiting at the house." Kumara Pillai replied, as he loaded their bags into the dickey of the car.

Seeing how crestfallen he was, Radha tried to help saying, "they probably wanted to give us some privacy, Prasad. We'll see them soon. Let us go."

Kumara Pillai nodded and started the car.

As they drove up the driveway, not a soul was visible. Disturbing thoughts flooded into Radha's mind. Did something happen to her achan? No! Kumara Pillai would have told her by now. If everybody was o.k. then where did they all go? Radha frowned. "Where is everyone?" She asked.

Before Kumara Pillai could answer, a deafening blast of fireworks from all around the house and an array of sparklers and floor crawlers on the driveway assaulted them. The front doors flew open and about twenty-five people, their close friends and relatives, streamed out, smothering them with hugs, and congratulating them on the great test results. Led by Kamala they sang in unison, "for he's a jolly good fellow---." Judge Menon's voice was heard the loudest, and even Lalitha, Prasad's Amma, joined in.

"So, good news travels fast?" Prasad wiped tears from his Amma's eyes.

He turned to Ammini Ammavi, "have you ever seen your Radha so happy? I think my remission has made her ecstatic, and I am pretty pleased about that."

Ammini Ammavi just hugged him. For once she was wordless.

Kamala took charge and hastened everybody into the house. A veritable feast awaited within.

"Chicken biriyani, my favorite. Thank you, Amma!" Prasad was excited.

"Thank Judge Menon, Prasad. He wished to serve all your favorite foods today. He even had the cook make your special tomato salad with onions and yogurt to go with the biriyani." His Amma smiled as she spoke.

Radha was touched. Her achan used to do such things when she was a girl. Since their fall out during her days with Danny, he had not been so spontaneous or generous. She looked at the table laden with food and saw more of Prasad's favorites. Prasad had a sweet tooth, and Radha was not aware that her achan had paid any attention to that. Yet, ada-payasam, made from rice noodles cooked slow and long in brown sugar, ghee, and coconut milk, was displayed in a large silver bowl, and she could even smell the touch of cardamom that laced it. She also saw the jilebis. Made from urad flour, they were shaped like mini-pretzels, but with umpteen more curves and coils than a usual pretzel. They were then soaked in sugar syrup with saffron, and having picked up the orange tint of the saffron powder, they added a bright spot in the layout.

Radha saw Prasad studying the abundant spread, and then walk away. She wondered where he was off to. She watched Prasad seek out her father and hug him. Both men were smiling broadly. She could not hear what they said to each other. The words did not matter. Her eyes filled with tears. Lord Krishna had finally brought her two men together.

When all the guests had left, Radha found her father in his library gazing at her Amma's portrait.

"Yes, achan, she would be very pleased you have come to care for Prasad. I am very grateful you are finally on my side again."

"Molé", he gathered her in a tight embrace and held her close. "I have always been on your side. It is just that my enthusiasm to protect you makes me blind to your feelings, sometimes. I am so sorry for all the years we spent disagreeing and arguing with each other."

Radha was silent in the warmth of his embrace, until she felt her father's tears on her face. She freed herself, and reached up with the loose end of her sari to wipe them. She had never seen his tears, even when her Amma died. She closed her eyes and remembered how stoic and detached her father had appeared then, while Ammini Ammavi, and Radha herself were cuddled close to her Amma's dead body, wailing hysterically and willing her to come back to them. For many years it had bothered her that her achan did not cry for her Amma.

She felt his eyes on her even before she turned around to see Prasad looking at her as he chatted happily with Ammini Ammavi. He smiled, and Radha murmured a prayer to Lord Krishna, to make the remission last. Then she walked over to Prasad and took his hand in hers.

As Radha made patient rounds the next morning, Dr. Mary Chacko peppered her with questions about the status of research and treatment of Adult Leukemia. Dr. Chacko was the Oncologist-Hematologist in charge of the Eastern research arm, in Trivandrum, of the Adult Leukemia Research of the University of Chicago. She herself was due to go to Chicago to study the progress of the project first hand, and to meet with her counterpart at the University of Chicago.

Six months passed by and Radha was thankful for the routine of her days with patient care, and nights with her family.

"What are you reading today, Radha?" Prasad's voice made her drop the magazine that she was reading. He had gone to visit his Amma at his sister's place, and Radha did not know that he had returned. She hurriedly picked up the magazine, and closed the page. "Catching up on all the progress in Medicine. She took his hand and tried to get him to the kitchen. "Let us go get a snack before we go to bed."

"I am not sleepy yet." Prasad answered. He took the magazine from her hand and flipped through the pages. "*Genetic changes following chemotherapy.* Is this what interested you?" He took her in his arms. "You are still thinking of the possibility of our having a child?"

He had hit the nail on the head. She did not answer.

"Radha dear, do you have any remorse of not having any children?" Prasad's spoke in a gentle voice.

"Of course I have pondered if we could have a child. But, no. I am not sorry. The data is quite unclear about the effects of the chemo on offsprings. And even if they have not found any problems so far, we should not take a chance on the chemo affecting a baby."

"Maybe we should not have married. I hate the fact that I am depriving you of the joys of motherhood."

"Look at me, Prasad. Do I look sad to you? I am so busy with my patients that I really don't have time to think about a baby. My practice and my family fill my life, and I truly am happy."

"But how about you dreams?"

Radha laid a finger on his lips. "No buts. We have each other, and that is all that matters. Let us be thankful for your remission, and enjoy our life as it is." With that she started towards the kitchen.

Prasad followed her.

I wonder how it would feel to hold your own newborn? I wonder if I could trust the child with others when I go to work? Will I ever be able to say no to my own child?

Radha's mind was still full of baby-thoughts, as she got ready for bed at night.

I am sure I would make a good mother. Fate has taken away my chances, and I have to make sure Prasad does not continue to feel guilty about it. I feel guilty enough that achan will not enjoy a grandchild from me. If my Amma were alive, maybe I would have thought of adopting a little one. Now achan will just have to settle for playing with Ammini Ammavi's grand-daughter, who is here often enough.

She sighed in relief when she saw Prasad deep in sleep when she got in bed and snuggled close to him.

A few months later Dr. Bob Bell called to say that he and Janice were getting married, and were planning a honeymoon in India. He wished to know if Radha and

Prasad would like to join them when they toured Delhi and Agra.

"I have always wanted to see the Taj Mahal in Agra." Radha was excited about the idea.

'I would love that also." Prasad agreed.

They coordinated the dates with Bob and Janice and met them in Delhi at the tail end of their honeymoon. Together they traveled to the city of Agra, mainly to see the Taj Mahal.

In Agra, as they unpacked in their hotel room, Prasad asked Radha, "Do you remember the beautiful piece that Tagore wrote about the Taj?"

"I'll find it." She said as she picked up her ever-present book by Tagore from her suitcase. She read aloud.

> " *This you perceived, O Shahjahan, Emperor of India,*
> *That life, youth, wealth and glory are swept away*
> *in the current of eternal Time.*
> *Only the anguish of his heart*
> *Be ever enduring - such was the striving of the Emperor*
> *The regal might as solid as the thunder*
> *Like the crimson hue of the sundown be merged into the*
> *depth of sleep, if so it be.*
> *Let one deep sigh*
> *Ever heaving, make the sky doleful-*
> *Such was the desire of your heart.*
> *Spleandour of diamonds, pearls, and rubies,*
> *Like diffusions of the rainbow,*
> *the illusion of the empty horizon*
> *Be effaced, if it must;*
> *Only abide,*
> *A drop of tear,*
> *Glistening white on the cheek of eternal Time -*
> *This Taj Mahal.*"

Tears streamed down both their cheeks and they embraced quietly.

They wished their first sighting of the Taj to be in moonlight. So, they had arranged their itinerary around the fourth phase of the moon. From the nearby village, they rode camels for the last one-mile of the trip. Motorcars are not allowed within one-mile radius of the Taj, to minimize damages to the marble mausoleum that was built in 1632, and one that took seventeen years to complete.

They walked through the fort, and coming down the dimly lit steps to the gardens in front of the Taj, they held hands and together looked up to see the white marble edifice in front.

There she lay glistening in the light of the full moon.

The central building of the mausoleum was built purely of white marble, and had a high dome on top. It sat elegantly poised atop a larger square platform of black and white marble in checkerboard design. The moonlight gave the Taj a silvery luster, and it glowed unlike any structure they had ever seen.

They held hands and cuddled close, as the guide explained how the Emperor Shah Jahan had built the Taj Mahal in memory of his wife Mumtaz Mahal (the Exalted of the Palace) who had died in childbirth. Even the experienced guide's voice faltered when he went on to tell the story of how close the emperor and his wife was, and how in her deathbed she asked the king to build a monument so beautiful that the world would never forget their love. He added how Shah Jahan had locked himself in his chambers for a whole month because he could not face the world devoid of his beloved.

Radha and Prasad hugged and cried silently, knowing that theirs too was an ill-fated match, with no 'long happy married life' to look forward to. They barely listened as the guide continued describing the four slender minarets, each one hundred and thirty feet high, were tilted away from the mausoleum so that in case of earth tremors they'd fall away from the building.

He pointed to the Agra Fort across the river Jamuna and added. "Their love story did not end there. The Emperor had installed a small crystal mirror, that reflected the Taj, outside his room. Years later, as he lay dying, he watched the Taj's reflection in it.

The tour continued, and all four marveled at the intricate inlaid designs in the marble and the guide read the inscriptions from the Quran that appeared on the entranceway. They were touched by the fact that the tomb of Shah Jahan was placed next to Mumtaz Mahal's tomb, and how his final resting place was beside his true love.

They walked outside and silently gazed at the Taj for a while longer.

"The Ultimate Monument of Love. A drop of tear glistening white on the cheek of eternal Time." Prasad murmured as they turned to leave. His voice was hoarse.

Another year passed, and there were no incidents and no problems with Prasad's health. Then, Prasad could not get over a common cold for more than ten days. Blood counts were still normal, but the type of cells seen in the blood smears showed trouble. Radha called Dr. Mary Chacko and she did a complete blood and bone marrow checkup on Prasad. It was, as Radha had feared, early signs that the leukemia was out of remission. After consulting with Dr. Bell, Dr. Chacko started a full course of chemotherapy. There was no need to go to Chicago anymore. The same treatments were available in Trivandrum.

While Prasad was in therapy, in the adjacent waiting room, Radha pondered over the events of the past few months. One evening, Radha's father, Judge Menon, was rushed to the hospital with chest pain. Tests showed that he had suffered a heart attack. Radha remembered how she had the best cardiologist in town come in to treat him. When they thought that he had stabilized and would recover, suddenly, unexpectedly, he developed heart failure and in spite of the best care that money could buy, he went into protracted failure and died in Radha's arms.

Radha shuddered at the sad memory. "After the tumultuous relationship with him all my adult life, we had finally made peace and were starting to be friends again, and you, Lord Krishna, took him away from me. Why is it that I hit these low valleys, just when I think I have conquered the last hill? I have just barely started to accept the fact that my achan is gone, and now you have given Prasad this set back. Why? Why are you testing my strength like this?"

Radha wished that her achan was there to console her now.

Despite all their differences, she had looked up to him for strength and stability in her life. Now she faced this crisis without him. She closed her eyes. She felt a gush of warm air and felt the pressure of his fingers on her hand. It was as if he was standing right beside her. She opened her eyes. She saw no one beside her. But she felt his presence and sighed. She looked up and silently thanked him for the sign of support at her time of need.

―――――――――

When Lalitha heard of Prasad's relapse, she moved back with Prasad and Radha to help take care of Prasad.

The treatments went on with the usual, expected, side effects of nausea, weakness and eventually, of losing his hair. Radha took a leave of absence from her practice to spend more time with him.

"Do you think Prasad need to go to Chicago to complete the treatments?' Lalitha asked Radha.

"No, Amma. The medicines are available here. We have to pray that they will work again, now." Radha answered. "As a matter of fact, the last tests show the abnormal cells all gone, and his normal cells on the increase."

"Does that mean he is in remission again?" His mother was anxious for good news.

"Not quite yet. But it seems that will happen soon." Radha consoled her.

A few weeks later, her prediction did come true. Prasad's leukemia was in remission again. But this time the chemo had taken its toll and he was too weak to go back to his firm and his practice.

Since Radha had to resume her duties at work, Lalitha stayed on to lift his spirit and to give Radha some peace of mind about his care while she was at work. Once Prasad regained his strength, Lalitha returned to her daughter's home.

Chapter Nineteen

If to leave this world be as real as to love it—
Then there must be a meaning in the meeting
and parting of life...
    Rabindranath Tagore

The big clock in the medicine department chimed
Seven. "Bhagavane´(oh, God), I am going to be late
for dinner at Kamala's once again." Dr. Radha spoke as she
turned to her assistant who was still adjusting the rate of
the medicines flowing into the I-V drip. The patient was
only 60 years old, but after his second episode of
myocardial infarction, he had suffered from heart failure,
and by now it was intractable. The patient had refused any
surgical intervention, and Radha was doing her best to get
him over the crisis.

"Dr. Sebastian, please take over for me, will you?
The patient's blood pressure is stable and I can be reached
at Dr. Kamala's house if you run into anymore problems."
She spoke in a voice firm enough to convince herself to
leave the hospital at last.

She removed her white doctor's coat, replaced her
stethoscope in her doctor-bag and closed the door behind
her.

"We have to hurry," she instructed Kumara Pillai, her chauffeur, as she settled down into the back seat of her car, "Prasad and I were expected at Dr. Kamala's for a dinner party at seven. I still have to get home and change before we can go to the party."

"Dr. Kamala will understand; you should not fret about it," Kumara Pillai consoled her. "If your patient turned critical there was nothing you could do to get away any earlier."

"Yes of course, I could not leave until his blood pressure was controlled and his heart condition stabilized."

"I am glad you did that." Kumara Pillai was always supportive. He had been her chauffer, and a good friend, for the longest time and was her sounding board, especially on a rough day, like the one she just had.

"Here; we are home, and safe. Now don't rush around and get yourself sick. I'll wait in the garden while you and Prasad get ready to go to the party." Kumara Pillai kept talking as he opened the car door for her, and took her doctor-bag from her, as she hurried into the house. "Hello, Prasad," she called out, looking up, towards their second floor bedroom. "I'll be ready in fifteen minutes. Sorry I am late!" She continued talking as she glanced through the messages on the antique ebony and brass table that was in the front reception hall. The house looked serene and welcoming. She glanced at her reflection in the mirror above the table. A gracious middle-aged lady, looked back from the mirror. She lifted her right hand and touched her temples, where a slight tinge of silver was starting to appear. She smiled to herself. Most of her friends were shocked when their silver strands first appeared. Radha realized that her first gray hairs did not bother her in the least.

"And why should it?" She spoke to herself. "My Amma did not live long enough to see her hair turn gray. I am fortunate to have Prasad in my life, and my patients are like family to me. It is true that I have suffered my share of pain. They say that the hottest fires forge the metal for the sharpest sword. I guess that now I am a sword ready to cut through any new challenge in my life."

She stopped perusing the mail. Something was missing; the house was too quiet. Usually when she got home, Prasad greeted her with, *"hello dear, how about a hot cup of tea?"* That was what was missing today. She peeked into the kitchen. It was empty. She called out again. "Prasad, where are you? Where is Madhavi?" The silence of the house echoed her question, and spread panic in her veins. Where was Prasad? What happened to Madhavi, her housekeeper? The mail and messages in her hands fell abruptly to the floor, and she bounded up the stairs to their bedroom, two at a time. Reaching the doorway to their bedroom, her heart stopped.

"Prasad!" Her voice quivered as she turned him over from where he lay face down, by the foot of their bed, and knew by his labored breathing and blue lips that something was quite wrong. She felt his brow; high fever. He had no fever when she said good-bye to him earlier that morning.

Prasad was trying to speak, but had trouble breathing, and no sound escaped. Radha knelt down and tried breathing into his mouth, and she realized he needed more help than she could offer at home. She could not understand why Prasad was alone at home. Where had Madhavi disappeared? She would have to find that out later.

Through the open window of the bedroom, she yelled down to Kumara Pillai for help. With their gardener's assist, they carried Prasad to her car. They rushed him to the University hospital. As Radha held his head on her lap, it felt burning hot, and her heart burned with the guilt of having left him alone. She murmured a prayer.

Once at the hospital, Prasad was placed on oxygen and intravenous fluids, and empiric antibiotic therapy was started. His temperature measured at 103 degrees. Chest X-ray showed flocculent shadows of pneumonic infiltration in both sides of the lungs. The white blood cell counts were elevated, but it was not a relapse of the leukemia; it looked more like an acute infection.

Radha watched as his breathing became regular and his flush from the fever subsided. She sighed with relief when he looked up at her and smiled. He still could not speak because the tubes from the respirator blocked his mouth. She felt his hand squeeze hers, and was not surprised at how weak he was. He had gone too long without enough oxygen at home with his belabored breathing, before she got him to the hospital.

Radha left the room and called Prasad's mother, who was with her daughter at the distant town of Palghat. When Radha filled them in on all the details of Prasad's condition, his sister promised Radha that she and her husband would try to get Amma to Trivandrum as soon as possible.

Prasad stayed in a feverish stupor all night, and Radha did not leave his bedside. With the early rays of the sun, she felt a soft touch on her shoulder. She must have dozed off, even in the uncomfortable chair in the room. Kamala was by her side, and she leaned down and silently hugged Radha. There was no need for words between two friends that knew each other better than they knew their own selves.

Prasad opened his eyes and Radha saw them well up with tears. He tried to talk, but a weak, hoarse, "I love you," was all he could muster.

"I love you too Prasad," Radha tried to keep her voice calm.

"Leukemia?" Prasad's weak mumbling expressed his concern that his Leukemia had relapsed. Radha understood.

"No, no. The leukemia is still in remission. You have developed pneumonia because of some infection. Dr. Mary Chacko is doing all the tests necessary to find out what kind of infection you have. Don't worry dear, they have started you on strong antibiotics to cover all the usual causes." Radha spoke to convince herself as much as to convince him.

She pulled up a chair sat down, and took his right hand in hers, to reassure him. Prasad slid back to sleep.

"The antibiotics have to work," she said to herself.

In the quiet of the sterile, almost colorless room, the silence only interrupted by the intermittent beeps of the monitor in the intravenous fluid pump, her whisper resounded, and startled her. She rose from her chair, gently placed his hand within his coverlets, and walked to the window. The sky was dark as far as she could see. Only a few stars kept vigil with her.

I will arrange an *archana*, sacred offering, for Lord Narayana at the temple tomorrow, in Prasad's name. I have to ask Ammini Ammavi to pick the pink oleanders, and maybe some roses from my garden to take to the temple. When the priest chants the thousand names of Lord Narayana for the *archana* on behalf of Prasad, he will need more than a thousand flower petals to offer at the deity's feet. Even if I can't be there, my flowers will carry my prayers to the Lord. What else can I do? All his medical needs are in the efficient hands of my colleagues. All I can do now is pray.

A day went by and the high fever still persisted. But Prasad seemed to breathe a little easier, and was not as restless as the day before. Kamala insisted that Radha go home to bathe and change and eat a proper meal, while Kamala stayed at the hospital with Prasad. She promised to call Radha immediately if anything changed.

"I hope you are not upset I left the house before you got home last night," Madhavi, their housekeeper was quite agitated and apologetic for leaving Prasad alone the previous night, when Radha had arrived to find him critically ill. "Since you both were planning to go to Dr. Kamala's last night, Prasad said I should go visit my daughter instead of staying here alone. When you were late in coming home, he insisted I leave before it got too dark. I am so sorry. I had no idea he was so ill."

"Of course you could not have known," Radha consoled her.

Alone in the large bedroom upstairs, Radha gazed vacantly at their empty bed, and she shuddered to think of what would have happened if she did not come home when she did.

In the shower she clutched the soap bar in her hand and she froze. What if the treatment they had started was not the right one? What if it is really too late? She shook herself free from the panic she felt. No. I have to believe the medicines will work. She quickly showered, lit an oil-lamp in her pooja room, and said all the prayers her confused mind could muster.

Then she called Ammini Ammavi and asked her to please not go to the Hospital to see Prasad, as yet. "Dr. Chacko wants to limit the number of visitors until she finds out the cause of the infection." Radha paused. "You can help us by going to the temple and have the priest do an archana for Prasad." She was relieved when Ammini Ammavi agreed. Radha could not bear to handle an overanxious Ammini Ammavi at Prasad's bedside.

She willed herself to eat a light meal before returning to the hospital, for fear of Kamala's wrath more than appeasing her own hunger. She had lost her appetite.

Dr. Mary Chacko met her at the hospital. "It looks like it might be Cytomegalovirus pneumonia. Special viral cultures are in progress. Since the results will not be ready for three days, I am placing Prasad on antiviral medicines."

"But that will hit him hard." Radha voiced concern.

"Yes it is some strong medicine we have to use. But, we really don't have a choice, Radha. If we delay therapy, we risk a progression of his pneumonia." Dr.Chacko placed a sympathetic hand on Radha's arm.

Radha knew the Cytomegalovirus is one opportunistic infection which was dreaded by all Oncologists. She needed reassurance, and called Dr. Bob Bell at the University of Chicago. He agreed with Dr. Chacko on starting the strong medicines.

Days passed, where his fever would go down for a while, and then up again, playing yo-yo with her feelings of hope and despair. Viral studies confirmed the Cytomegalovirus infection. Once she made sure all that was humanly possible was being done for Prasad, Radha settled down by Prasad's bed with her bible, the *Bhagavad Geetha*, and her book of poetry, *Gitanjali* by Tagore.

As Radha watched the multiple tubes entering his tired hot body, she remembered the first time she laid eyes on him. She remembered how, despite the foreboding she had felt at that time, their lives had entwined in this wonderful knot of love and caring for the past eight years. They had licked his leukemia, and even more importantly, they had overcome the fear it brought with it, to go on living a fulfilling life. She could not imagine how she would have survived her father's death if Prasad had not been there for her.

Prasad opened his eyes. Radha put on a brave smile, and wiped her eyes. His voice was weak as he spoke. "Radha dear, don't let Amma see your tears. Unlike you and me she is not strong and will not be able to handle the finality of my illness."

"Don't give up yet, Prasad." She had to be brave for him even though she trembled with fear inside. "Of course I will not let Amma see me upset. Let me ask her to come in now." Radha rose from her chair.

"Wait, Radha." Prasad stopped her. "I have to talk to you before you get Amma. . ." He had to catch his breath.

"You will have plenty of time for that, dear." She tried to be convincing.

"No. Radha dear, I want to make sure I say this to you now. I want you to remember you have been my beacon in the dark and," he had to pause for his breath, "Radha, I love you."

Radha sat down again, tears streaming down her face.

"How can I leave this good life I have with you so soon?" A sob interrupted his words. "While I can still talk, I am asking you to stop pining for me when I am gone, and go on with your life."

"No--no!" She protested and silenced him with a kiss. She was not ready for his good-byes. "I am certain the antiviral therapy will kick in soon and you will recuperate in no time at all. You will have plenty of time to tell me all these mushy things I love to hear and you hate to say. Save your energy and fight the infection, darling. I'll be right here for you."

"Radha, I can feel it. I feel weak and beaten." He spoke in short sentences, now. "I know I only have a short time left."

Radha could not hold back the tears. It was not the first time she had heard similar words from patients who would be seemingly improving in their medical conditions, but once they had lost the will to live, no medications would render the desired effect, and they would go downhill pretty quickly. Panic struck her and it took all her self-control to speak smoothly. "Amma is now waiting outside and I'll bring her in. After you visit with her let me know if you want to speak to your sister and brother-in-law."

Outside Prasad's room, Radha explained to Amma how he was feeling quite dejected and pessimistic. She led Amma to Prasad's bedside, and went out to find the rest of the family.

Radha explained to Prasad's sister, brother-in-law, and Ammini Ammavi how the therapies had not brought the fever down and how low he was feeling. She had a hard time convincing them that transferring him to the University of Chicago would not alter any of the therapy, and that all the medicines needed were available right there, at home.

With Kamala's help, Radha had barely calmed down the three of them, when Amma came out and hysterically announced to everyone that Prasad had requested that all feeding and oxygen tubes be removed and that he wanted to say goodbye to the rest of the family.

Radha rushed in--"Prasad, what craziness is this? You need the support of the full, heavy therapy to beat this infection. Don't, oh please don't give up now."

"I'll never give up on you dear, but I know it is time to go. I want to bid goodbye to everyone while my mind is still clear." He paused. "No more tubes. The Lord beckons. All I want now is you by my side."

Radha had to give in. She arranged with Dr. Chacko to discontinue all heroics. Kamala stood by her teary-eyed friend, arranging for each member of the family to go in and pay final respects.

Finally, she was alone with him.

Prasad insisted that she read from the final chapters of Tagore's writings. Between sobs she read...

There are numerous strings in your lute,
Let me add my own among them
Then when you smite your chords
My heart will break the silence
And my life will be one with your song.

The words were written by Tagore in his own last days and were addressed to Lord Krishna, referring to Krishna's flute and metaphorically welcoming the end of mortal life to attain salvation in becoming one with the Lord and his music.

As she glanced up from the pages, she saw he too was crying. Prasad's eyes met hers and he reached a feeble arm towards her. She dropped the book and sat close to him holding his hand in hers. His voice was weak as he spoke.

"Dear --, let me say goodbye. You're the best thing that happened to me."

"Stop, Prasad, don't try to talk." She interrupted, seeing how difficult it was for him to speak.

Prasad shook his head. "I will be watching you from the high post near Lord Krishna. Don't cry ... take care ... " He had to stop.

Radha held him close.

Prasad whispered again. "Your prayers, Radha. I want to hear ... the Lord's name."

"Narayanam bhaje´ narayanam
Lekshmi narayanam bhaje´ narayanam ..."
Radha prayed, chanting the familiar words softly through sobs and tears.

Her voice trailed off where sobs took over and she dropped to the side of his bed and held him close as he mumbled softly "narayana ... narayana ...", and his arms encircling her body, as she leaned over him, were weak and feeble. Soon she felt his breathing belabored, and she felt his arms lose their grip on her shoulder as he breathed his last.

Prasad's brother-in-law made all the arrangements for the funeral. As was the custom among Hindus, the cremation took place before the next sundown.

Prasad's body was laid out in their living room, outfitted in a simple white shirt and mundu, a Sarong-like South Indian outfit. An oil lamp with seven wicks was lit, and placed by his head, and a smaller lamp by his feet. Family and friends came to say good-bye, laying flowers at his head and feet. The immediate family, and close relatives honored him with drapes of red silk and white muslin, to cover the body, symbolizing a colorful life and a simple departure.

Radha and Ammini Ammavi sat on the floor, by the right side of his body, and his mother and sister were to his left. Each time a friend or an uncle came to place flowers, the women's voices rose in wails, many times uncontrollable. A few women sat at the corner of the room chanting Ramayana, the story of Rama, one of Vishnu's incarnations.

It was time for the blessing of the body, before the trip to the cremation grounds. Through her daze, Radha heard fragments of familiar verses from the *Bhagavat Geetha*, The song of the Lord, being chanted by the priest. From her religion studying days as a young girl, she recognized the advice given by Lord Krishna, another of Vishnu's incarnations in the *Geetha*.

The Hindus believe that the *Atman*, or soul, is
immortal, even after the perishable body has been shed. In
one's earthly existence, one accumulates *desires and
attachments* that detract from the absolute truth that the
Atman is immortal. This causes *Karma,* which is the *duty*
that has to be fulfilled due to the *desires* that the *Atman* has
accumulated. The *Atman* is reborn in a different form and
place to fulfill the *Karma*. Thus the cycle of birth and
rebirth continues, accompanied by all the mortal miseries
and pain that accompany such lives.

The verses in the *Geetha* consist of advice from Lord
Krishna as to how one can live in this world without
desires and attachments, dedicating all actions in the name
of God Almighty. This will stop the accumulation of
Karma. Then the realization will come that one's *Atman*
and the *Divine power* of God Almighty are one and the
same. When this enlightenment happens, the *Atman*
attains the divine status of *Nirvana,* an absolute state of
oneness with God Almighty, stopping the cycle of birth
and rebirth, and thus escaping mortal miseries and pain
forever.

The life of a true *Hindu* is considered a quest
towards this state, and his/her mission is to strive towards
Nirvana.

None of the chanting made any sense to Radha at
this time of unbearable pain.

The cremation grounds were a few miles from the
house and the male members of the family and friends
present accompanied the body in procession. Neither
Radha, Amma, nor any other female member of the family
attended the funeral, in deference to the custom of only
men taking the body to the funeral pyre.

"I am glad you decided not to go with them."
Kamala said, as she helped Radha to put out the oil lamps
that had been lit by Prasad's body. Within a house of

mourning the oil lamp will remain unlit, even for prayers, for a period of five days. They sat huddled together with Prasad's sister and said prayers invoking Lord Narayana to take the departed soul to His very bosom.

Ammini Ammavi was in bed, in the next room. She had fainted when the body was being taken away, and a few women sat by, tending to her. Sleep was late in coming for all of them that night. Radha would not go to bed. Kamala stayed by her side through the night.

"What did I do wrong, Kamala?" Between her quiet weeping and her sobs, Radha asked. "Should I have taken him to Chicago for treatments, again?"

"No, Radha. You did all that needed to be done. Prasad was ready to go. You had to let him go. Now you have to accept the fact that he is gone."

Radha sat up straight. "Do you think that my old love for Danny haunted our lives, and made Prasad lose his will to live?"

Kamala took a firm hold of both her shoulders, and looked into Radha's eyes. "Listen to me. I have known you all your life, and got to know Prasad quite well. He did not give up living because of any ghosts from the past. I don't think you should feel any guilt for what fate did to you and Prasad. He knew you loved him completely."

Through the long night Kamala tried to calm and to console Radha. Finally, towards the early hours of dawn Radha fell into a restless sleep and Kamala also laid down to sleep.

A couple of hours passed. Radha started screaming uncontrollably. Kamala shook her gently, saying, 'Radha wake up. Wake up Radha." She tried to ease Radha out of whatever nightmare that she was having.

Finally, Radha opened her eyes and looked up in bewilderment. "Kamala, I was walking with Prasad on the sandy shores of a calm ocean, and a great big storm rose up and the waves engulfed us. As suddenly as it started, the storm disappeared, leaving me alone on the beach, wet and alone, searching for Prasad." She sat up and looked around in a daze. "Why are you here Kamala? Where is Prasad?" She woke up in a scary sweat, her confusion replaced by the shocking reality of the day before.

Kamala held Radha tight and rocked her in her arms till her sobbing stopped and Radha was completely awake. There were no words in Kamala's vocabulary to console her friend. She just held her till the tears flowed to dryness and Radha slipped back into a restless sleep.

Later that morning Radha woke up and asked to see Amma. She hugged and kissed Lalitha, and apologized profusely for not being able to find a cure for her son. Surprisingly, Amma was the strong one.

"Mol, just think of how happy you made Prasad for the past seven and a half years." Lalitha took Radha's hands and held them tight imparting some of her strength to Radha. "If it were not for your love and hope, I myself would not have enjoyed the past few years with my son. Now it is time for us both to say goodbye to him and to pray to our Lord Narayana for peace for Prasad's soul."

In the afternoon Kamala convinced Radha to freshen up and have a cup of hot tea. After tea, Radha was in her dressing room combing her hair, and reflexively reached out for her red dot to place the *thilakam* on her forehead. Sudden realization paralyzed her. She was a widow. She would not be wearing a *thilakam* anymore.

It was an old Hindu custom that starting at an early age Hindu girls wore a circular dot of black or red in the center of their forehead. It represented all that was good in life and it was also customary that this dot, called *thilakam*, was not worn by any person in mourning and not at all by widows. As the shock of that reality hit her, she was in tears again. Why did you leave me so soon? She talked to Prasad, knowing fully well that he was not there.

She refused food or drinks for the rest of the day, and remained in a state of confusion and denial despite Kamala's heroic efforts.

The next morning Prasad's brother-in-law brought the burnt remains of the body in a *kalasam*, brass jar. The *kalasam* with Prasad's ashes was placed under a mango tree in her front yard. Such remains were never brought into the house.

As part of the special rituals of mourning, an oil lamp was lit near the kalasam holding the ashes, and the vigil for the safe journey of the spirit to the *Akasic abode*, in the ethereal space beyond our earthly existence, began.

During this period, special rites were held in honoring the departed soul, and to release the soul from human bondage.

Three days later, Kamala broached the subject of Radha returning to work. "I could not care for my own; how could I care for my patients?" Radha was hard on herself. "I don't want to think of medicines, procedures or patients any more."

Kamala shook her head. She made arrangements with their colleagues to cover Radha's practice and scheduled a leave of absence from her teaching job. Nothing Kamala or Amma could say would induce Radha to return to her patients. Her feeling of guilt that her knowledge of medicine, nor all her friends in the sub-specialties of medicine could help Prasad, had rocked the core of her confidence in the system. She roamed around the house in a bewildered state and seldom spoke to anyone. For the most part they left her alone. It took all of their combined efforts to make sure that she ate at least one meal a day and that too under protest.

Radha herself was unsure what she would do next.

Chapter Twenty

Now I am waiting on the seashore to feel thee in death;
to find life's refrain back again in the star-songs of the night
                    Rabindranath Tagore

Three weeks had passed since Prasad died.

There was a knock at her bedroom door, and when Radha opened it, there stood her old friend Manohar. Radha turned her head away from him and sobbing uncontrollably muttered, "Manohar, go away, I do not wish for you to see me in this state. Why did you come?"

"Kamala and Ammini Ammavi are quite worried about you. They have never seen you in such a state of despair and are afraid you will get sick from this sad state you are in."

"I too deserve to die." She was defiant. "I could not do enough to save Prasad. Why should I go on living?"

"You have to go on living because it is not your time to go, yet. You have to go on living because Amma needs you, and your patients need you." He stepped into her room and took her hand. "Come on out and I want you to meet somebody."

After much coaxing Radha came out of her room and down the stairs to the living room. There on the floor sat a little girl, playing with a baby doll, combing the doll's hair and crooning softly to her. A young lady, whose face was not familiar to Radha, sat watching her. Radha looked up at Manohar.

The question in her eyes was answered by Manohar. "Amidst all your calamitous past three years I purposely avoided telling you about my family. Meet Vaani my wife and Renu our pride and joy. I thought it might make you feel good to see I did take your advice and decided to get on with my life."

The baby girl, about two years old, lifted her cherubic face and smiled at Radha, as if she had known her all her life. Then, she lifted the doll and offered it to Radha. Radha sat down beside her and gathering her in her arms, spoke softly. "Renu. A beautiful name for a beautiful girl." The little girl reached up and touched Radha's curly hair. Radha's face lit up. She rose from the floor, holding the baby and said hello to the mother.

Radha was distracted long enough to get herself out of the rut she was in. "Has anybody gotten any food for you all?" Manohar and family had just arrived from Bombay, and her immediate instinct was to take care of their needs. She walked back to the kitchen to arrange for their comforts and would not hear of them leaving without having eaten supper. She fussed over the baby and for the first time since Prasad's death, took interest in what was happening in her world.

Manohar, Vaani and Renu returned to Bombay,after a week of effective distraction, and the house was filled with gloom again.

Radha ate a light supper and went up to her bedroom. A few minutes later Lalitha knocked on her door. "Can I come in?"

"Yes, of course." Radha opened the door promptly. As sad or upset that she was she would not think of keeping Prasad's mother waiting at her door.

"What time are you planning to go to the hospital in the morning? I would like to come along, if you don't mind, and give my thanks to the nurses who took care of Prasad."

"I am not sure I am going in tomorrow." Radha said, but without the stubbornness or conviction she had felt in the weeks prior to Manohar's visit.

Lalitha sat on Radha's bed and looked up at Radha. Her eyes were moist. "Prasad, my son, loved you deeply and would not want you wasting your knowledge and your spirit, pining away for him. He would want you to go out there and take care of your patients. I also wish you would do the same, please."

Radha walked over to the window and stood gazing at the sky.

Lalitha got up from the bed, went to her and put her arms on Radha's shoulders.

"What do you say? Let us plan on leaving about 8:30 in the morning. For tomorrow, just review the patient charts in your service. I'll wait in your office until you are done, and we will return home together."

Radha turned around and hugged her. "You will do this for me? It will certainly make it easier for me to resume my work at the hospital; yes, I'll try to start tomorrow."

The next morning Radha returned to her ward and her charts. Her first day was kept short. The residents and nurses curbed their questions to allow her return home by noon.

It did not take too long for all her patients to come back, and soon she was busy practicing medicine again.

Two months passed quickly.

One afternoon Lalitha got a call from her daughter in Palghat. She was going to have surgery done on her hand, and asked if her mother could go there to help her with her children.

"Amma, you should go to her. I am o.k. now." Radha's voice was firm.

"I know she can get someone else to help if I don't go. You still need me here, I think." Lalitha was not so sure.

"I want you to be there for her. I will be all right. Ammini Ammavi and Kamala will watch me closely, and I promise to take care of myself. With the two of them around you won't have to worry." Radha was almost jovial.

She convinced Lalitha to go and be with her daughter.

A few weeks later Dr. Sebastian, Radha's assistant received orders to transfer to a Government hospital and had to leave immediately. It took over a month to get his replacement in place, and Radha had no choice but to see a full load of patients and make rounds twice a day with her residents. The exhausting schedule was a real boon to Radha; it afforded her no time to dwell on the constant ache which persisted in her heart for Prasad.

Kamala checked up on her at their usual 10 a.m. coffee breaks at The Canteen. Set in the center of the campus, The Canteen had been their gathering place forever for coffee or light meals, and also to celebrate birthdays, passing exams or winning bets. But above all it was at the Canteen that they made momentous decisions of their youth as to which sari to wear to a party, or if they both would attend a party, or snub the party-giver. Now they met there to rejoice when a critical patient came out of the woods, or to cry on the other's shoulder when either one lost her patient to fate.

One such morning as they sat sipping hot coffee, Kamala asked. "Will you make it to Bindu's birthday party next week?" Kamala's daughter was turning twelve, and Radha had missed more than one of her birthday celebrations while caring for Prasad, and because of her travels to Chicago.

Radha sensed the reservation in Kamala's voice, as if she did not want to push Radha into going to the party. Radha laughed.

"Kamala, you don't have to be hesitant. Yes. I am going. No. Prasad's absence will not keep me from coming to Bindu's party. I have promised myself not to miss out on any of her celebrations ever again. She is my favorite niece."

"What is going on? You sound like you have something happening with you to lift your spirits."

"You may say that!" There was excitement in Radha's voice. "Dr. Srinivasan and his group from the Cancer Center Implementation Committee stopped by and asked me to be on the Board. The Cancer Center building is nearing completion, and they are hoping to furnish, complete staff selection and define programs within the next year. Dr. Bob Bell from the University of Chicago nominated me."

"What a great idea! I hope you agreed to be on the Board. You will be a great asset."

"I don't know, Kamala, I am not so certain. Even if I did not join the Board, I am going to stay active with the Center. I am setting up a scholarship fund in Prasad's name for a Fellow in Leukemia Research. I have convinced Prasad's Amma to go in on it with me.

"Does it make you sad, Radha?" Kamala reached forward and squeezed Radha's hand.

"Yes. In many ways it makes me sad. I do so miss him. He was kind and caring and had accepted me as I was. I am sad I could not get him appropriate therapy for a cure. I miss him very much Kamala."

"Radha, dear, you know Prasad would have wanted you to be on the Board. Having gone through the pain with him, your insight will be very valuable in setting up protocols for research and treatment."

"You are right, Kamala. I should be honored I am offered this opportunity to do some good."

Radha took Kamala's advice and contacted Dr. Srinivasan. As much as Radha's input was valuable to setting up the program, her involvement was more gratifying to Radha herself than she had imagined.

At the end of the year, the Grand Opening of The Cancer Center was announced. In conjunction with the official Inauguration Ceremonies, there were many conventions arranged. *The Student and Faculty Alumni Association* was in charge of organizing the programs, both the scientific sessions as well the social and fund-raising events. Conventions where in progress in different parts of the city and suburbs of Trivandrum. Experts from all over the world were participating and sharing information on the Status of research regarding the etiology of the various cancers affecting different organs. Also panel discussions were held about testing for early diagnosis of tumors. Regarding treatments, both medical and surgical groups were gathered in many different auditoriums, debating the efficacy of the different modalities, separately and in combination, and comparing survival statistics and the effectiveness of such treatments.

Radha was asked to host the group that was holding the meetings at the Kovalam Beach Resort for that particular weekend. She had completed all the arrangements and she attended some of the sessions regarding treatment of breast cancer. A small group of friends urged her to join them for a swim. It had been a long three days of meetings and discussions and she felt she needed to unwind. So she joined them.

As they dunked each other, and shared memories of the past with old friends, some of whom she was seeing after many years of separation, Radha felt years shed away. She laughed and joked wholeheartedly, for the first time since Prasad had died. She felt that in helping to complete the project of the Cancer Center, and launching its functions, she had paid tribute to a husband and friend, and done what could be done to immortalize him.

Chapter Twenty One

My heart today smiles at its past night of tears
Like a wet tree glistening in the sun
After the rain is over
        Rabindranath Tagore

Radha looked up from the water and saw his face in silhouette up on the balcony. Her heart stopped. Oh no! It cannot be him. But, she saw that it was. She had known his name was on the list of guest lecturers, but had purposefully avoided all meetings and discussion groups he would be participating in, in the past three days. She had been successful thus far. He turned around and their eyes met. He ran down the steps to the beach and called out to her. "Is that really you, Dr. Radha? I have been looking all over for you. Where have you been hiding?" He sounded like any other acquaintance, meeting after twenty years.

Radha swallowed hard. She could not speak because her heart was beating so fast she was out of breath. Her mouth felt dry, although she was soaking wet. Slowly she walked out of the water and grabbed her towel. Wrapping herself in it she walked towards him. Controlling her voice, she extended her hand and spoke softly. "Hello Danny."

Radha saw his smile fade, possibly responding to the pain he saw in her face.

Dropping his casual demeanor, he spoke in a serious tone. "Can we go in and talk?" She nodded yes. She turned to make her excuses to her friends in the water and side by side, they walked up to the beach resort. He found them a table away from the crowds and they sat down. In spite of the hot afternoon sun, she trembled. He ordered her a cup of hot tea. He walked around the table and gently gathered her beach towel tighter around her.

And then they started to talk. But where do you find words adequate to tell each other all that happened in twenty years? They kept stumbling on each other's sentences, and her tears kept choking much of what she tried to say. Mutual friends stopped by to say hello, thus interrupting even the barest stream of conversation they could muster. They finished their tea. She said in a hesitant faltering voice. "I have a suite in this hotel. Can we go up there and talk?" He nodded acquiescence and they both went up to her suite.

It was there in the veranda adjoining her suite that she sat by him all afternoon, each filling the other in on all the happenings of their lives for the past twenty years.

Radha learned Danny had completed Surgery Residency and joined a well-known Surgeon in Delhi. "For many years after we separated I was not myself. I immersed myself in my surgery practice. Then I met and married a co-surgeon, who after two years of marriage and one daughter decided that her career took precedence over us. I felt our daughter Sheenu was better off being with my mother in Cochin. She had a more stable life, going to school there, than being cared by nannies or placed in some impersonal boarding schools. Later, Sheenu's mother and I did get divorced and I have lived a bachelor life since then."

Radha told him all about her practice. She also told him how she had met and married Prasad, and about Prasad's demise. She told him how she was involved with the Cancer center project and how she had accepted a position on the Board. She confided in Danny that perhaps her enthusiasm for the work came partly from her sense of loss resulting from Prasad's death.

The afternoon passed quickly. All the main events had been told and they were back to the present. A somber mood settled upon them.

The evening sun blazed streaks of orange-red fire over the rising emerald waves in the Indian Ocean. As the waves waned and hit the beach, their fire spread out on the foam, each bubble burning its last bright ember as they died and disappeared on the white and tan grains of sand.

Radha felt her whole being tense up, as Danny slid down from his chair and kneeling beside her gazed up into her eyes. Her eyes brimmed with tears. Like dark sapphires set before a glowing fire, the anger that rose behind them made them sparkle sharply for a fleeting moment.

Danny picked up her book of Tagore from the teapoy beside them and flipped through the pages, and read with an ease bred of long-term familiarity:

My heart, the bird of wilderness, has found its sky in your eyes.
They are the cradle of the morning, they are the kingdom of the stars.
My songs are lost in their depths.
Let me but soar in that sky, in its lonely immensity.
Let me but cleave its clouds and spread wings in its sunshine.

So, he still knew her favorite poems. Radha turned her face away from him.

"Don't look away from me, now."

The pleading in Danny's voice took her by surprise and soon a wave of strong feelings for him surged up from within the deep oceans of her heart, where they had lain dormant for many years, and shining through her moist eyes covered him in a worshipping moonlight of soothing love.

"Radha," Danny's voice was hoarse with dense emotion. "When I saw you earlier in the water, all the past years slipped away and you were the same nineteen year old that I have carried around in my heart. Your curly hair, sparkling wet in the sunshine, tugged at the very core of my heart, and the pain was unbearable! The pain of realization that in letting you go I cheated us both of the joy of our love for so long." He laid down his head upon her lap.

"No...Danny...no!" Radha was moved to protest his guilt-laden tirade on himself. But, she did not know what else to say. The professor with an enviable vocabulary, the doctor who had loads of advice for her patients, always, the fun-loving friend who had a pocketful of jokes for all occasions, now was at a loss for words. No words could express all the love that had remained bottled up in her, in a remote alcove of her heart, an alcove containing a grotto where he had lain enshrined for many years. It was a grotto that she had locked up with a rock of determination. She had planned never to open it. Never held any hope to open it! Now, his hand touching hers, his honest admission of an error made twenty years ago, the sharp edge in his hoarse voice as he spoke, broke the seal and moved the rock. The shrine lay open. The grotto, once dark and bleak, now lit by the light of his love, revealed to him his own self enshrined. No force of fate could take away from them this moment of honesty.

The sounds of breaking surf brought her back to earth.

"Danny, how can you go on like this? You left me once and how do I know what your plans are now? How can I trust our love, after what we went through then?"

"Maya," he called her by his special endearment from the past. Maya- illusion or magic. He stopped abruptly and corrected himself. "Radha, do you think that I would have left Trivandrum and you to go to Delhi if you had given me any glimmer of hope for a future together? You gave me no reason…no hope to stay around. I thought it was best to leave. Thought it was best to get as far away from you as possible, for your sake more than mine, Maya. I would give up half my life to undo the past; to turn back the clock, if I only could, and relive all those years with you."

"It devastated me to deny us our love." Radha interrupted him. "Not that my sacrifice had been in vain! I did what I did then, for my father, to whom I was the Earth, Moon and Stars all rolled up into one."

"That was then, Maya, we are here now, and please don't rob us of this second chance that has been offered us."

Radha shook her head.

"Give us a chance, Maya. *Oyyire koduthum ommaye naan kaapeen,* (I promise to protect you with my life), the words from your favorite song, Maya..." his voice trailed into a sob. The pleading in his voice broke down her defenses, totally.

There was no power on earth that could harness the strength of her love for him anymore. With both of her arms she lifted his head up from her lap, gently lowered her face and placed her lips to his. He raised himself up and pulled her up with him, and as they both stood, and before either one of them knew what was happening, they ended up in a tight embrace.

"Twenty years of longing for this moment, and I never once thought that this would be possible again."

Danny muttered, as he buried his face into her hair, kissing
the nape of her long graceful neck, again and again.

They trembled at the realization that they finally,
held each other in their arms. There was no stopping now.
He gently moved her curly hair away from her eyes, and
seeing the shades of gray at her temples, stroked them,
tenderly. A wave of longing swept through her body.
Turning, her lips brushed lightly at the tip of his luscious
beard. In the past, the same beard, along with his long hair,
had been condemned by her father as being unsuitable in
any man who would dare woo his precious daughter. She
shuddered as all the pain from her past came flooding in
along with the memories, and Danny felt her drifting away
from him even as he held her in his arms.

He stopped kissing and lifted her face up to his.
"Have you not suffered enough? Have we not paid in tears
for all those years apart? Maya, we deserve to be happy.
We deserve our love to be given a chance. Let's not deny us
the happiness of our time together, at last. Please don't
punish us for our past mistakes."

Hesitantly, she looked up at him and allowed her
tense body to relax. Radha closed her eyes and let his
words sink in, finally acknowledging to herself the truth in
his arguments. Danny was right. No, now was not the time
for regrets. For once her longing for him and their love for
each other were winning over logic and common sense.
She led him slowly to her bedroom.

The lamps were not lit yet, and the first rays of
moonlight were streaming in through the open windows.
The sound of the waves was rhythmic, providing an apt
background to the real music that now swelled in their
hearts. Passion surged, and caught up in its tidal wave,
they were engulfed in one glorious act of love.

Later, the sound of the waves lapping on the sands
seemed calmer, slower, as though the energy of the storm

was spent up, even as their fervor was exhausted. The soothing, calm moonlight now shone fully on them, the wet winds wafted from the sea to cool them, and the soft music of the waves lulled them into a deep sleep. Even as she fell asleep, comfortably cradled in the safety of his strong yet gentle arms, she murmured. "Tomorrow! I'll worry about the consequences tomorrow!"

Chapter Twenty Two

Mirth spreads from leaf to leaf, my darling,
and gladness without measure.
The heaven's river has drowned its banks
and the flood of joy is abroad.
  Rabindranath Tagore

The sun came up to see the two of them still in bed. The orange hues and the gentle breezes of the night before were replaced by a white blazing summer sun glaring through the window, and a hot wet breeze rustled the white lace curtains.

Radha woke up and saw Danny still fast asleep by her side. A happy, content smile played upon his face. His hair fell softly on his temples like the gentle waves of a calm sea. Memories of the previous night brought a smile to her face.

With his first passionate kiss, Danny had awakened in Radha emotions that had lain asleep for the longest time. Her soft supple body tensed up with passion to his tender caresses. Gently and unhurriedly he removed her robe and slipped down the straps of her swim-suit. He uttered no words. Instead his eyes spoke volumes, and Radha saw in them the love he felt towards her. His fingers spoke its language of love to her body, and as she felt Danny's passion aroused, so too her body responded to his missives, and they had united in a joy that neither had believed possible to share in the present lifetime. It was night of unrestrained expression of true love for both.

"The tomorrow I worried about, is upon me now," she mused. "What do we do now? Was last night just a left over emotion from all those years apart, or is it the true love I had imagined we had shared all those years ago?" She was well aware of the commitments the two of them had at different parts of the country. She knew they were not the young medicos whose dreams were once shattered on the rocks of time. Were they too old to build their own dream-castles again?

She was deeply immersed in her thoughts and did not know Danny was awake, until she turned around and saw him gazing at her longingly. Their eyes met.

Danny leaned over and touched her face tenderly, and spoke. "I am not certain this is not a dream, *omané*, (darling); a dream I have dreamt more than once after I lost you. Maya, I am afraid to move lest I will chase away the vision of beauty I see in front of me. I am afraid I'll break the spell and chase away the rainbow I see in my sky after so long a rainy season".

Radha silently pressed her body closer to him and kissed him fully in the mouth. She was not an illusion. Her silence and her bodily motions only enhanced his need for her and their passions aroused once again, they found fulfillment in each other's arms. Thus united, they went back to sleep fully ignoring the rest of the world like only true lovers can.

Later, when they were awake, Danny reached over and pulled her close. "I can see the worry in your eyes. Are you thinking where this is leading us? In all our years apart I knew that I loved you, but had never imagined how strong my feelings are for you, until last night. I now know what I have to do."

He swiftly got out of their bed, and kneeling down, took her hands in his. "Maya, you have been my illusion so far. Will you marry me? Will you become my reality and make my dreams come true?"

"Oh Danny," Radha closed her eyes letting the meaning of his words sink in. "Don't we have to iron out a few wrinkles before I can even consider any answer?"

"Oh, please", he pleaded hoarsely, "say yes, and I promise you I shall give up all I have, to be with you for the rest of our lives."

"How about your life and work in Delhi? How about your patients? How about your daughter?"

She was silenced by his kiss.

"Radha, my *omané*", she knew he was serious when he addressed her by her real name rather than Maya. "First tell me that you will marry me. We can address all the problems together and come up with solutions."

Oh Danny, I- I don't know what to say."

"Say yes my omané," Danny insisted.

"I will marry you my love." Tears of happiness flowed freely, giving her face a wet glow in the morning sun.

"Omané," Danny wiped away her tears. "I am sure many have said these words before me, but none have been more sincere when I say that you have made me the happiest man on earth." His big brown eyes sparkled with renewed hope and excitement.

Now Radha was up and both sat side by side, holding each other.

"As far as my career," Danny spoke firmly, "just last night the Professor of Surgery had asked me to head the Surgical Oncology Unit at the new Cancer Center. I had told him that I did not think that it was plausible, but that I would give him a final answer soon. I'll see if the offer still stands."

"But, you would be starting your career all over again dear, and I really cannot ask you to do that. A new Hospital, a new Surgical unit and a totally new Surgical team; there are bound to be many problems. You will be expected to be diplomatic in your management. There is so much politics in play, and I know it will be difficult for you to tolerate all that. How can I ask you to put up with such drastic changes?"

"For you my darling, I shall lay myself down to die."

She could not find any more excuses, not that she really needed them. "Yes, Danny I'll marry you," Radha murmured, as she snuggled up close to him and closed her eyes tightly, to shut out any more problems that may come up.

The various meetings and lectures, and dealing with the many of the other guests kept them busy the rest of the morning.

The afternoon heat prompted them to cool off in the ocean. Getting out of the water, Radha turned towards him. "Danny, do you know how I feel right now?" Danny's face broke out into the widest of smiles, at how happy Radha's voice sounded.

"No! I really think you should show me." He ran to her, his feet sinking and faltering in the sands making any quick approaches impossible. He tried to grab her close to him and plant a kiss on her laughing lips.

Wisely she put out her hands and held him in abeyance. "You can't do this in public. It might be 1990s, but I am still Prasad's widow and we know very well that in this town it is not a good idea to kiss and carry on in public. Also we both know there are a million cobwebs spun by the unsettled issues of our past that we need to face and conquer, yet."

"Radha, I am elated we have decided to seize this second chance at a life together. Our love rekindled, I feel very valiant and confident about our facing any obstacles that life would throw our way now." He took her arms and led her to a shady spot under the waving coconut palms affording a mild relief from the hot tropical sun.

When the cool breezes picked up for the evening, and the sun's rays were slanting down, they ventured out for a walk on the sands. Soft white clouds chased across the blue skies with abandon and helped lighten their hearts just by their presence.

Hand in hand they walked by the edge of the sea, oblivious to admiring glances, and some curious, raised brows from ones who knew their previous history. But fortunately for Radha, they did not stop to talk to the pair; until they came upon Kamala and her husband, Biju.

"We know all about you, and are so happy that you are both together finally." Kamala was exuberant. "When we get back to Trivandrum, I want you to come and stay with us, Danny. I know it is going to be awkward to stay at Radha's house and we don't want you going to a hotel."

"Oh no, I would not want to impose." Danny protested.

"You don't have a choice, Danny, there is no way that I am going to give you a chance to back out now. I am keeping a close surveillance on you to make sure that my friend here stays happy. So, you are staying with us. That's it. Case closed." Kamala was insistent.

Danny threw up his hands in defeat. "I'll be very happy to accept your invitation. But you really don't have to worry about my disappearing again. I am older and hopefully wiser. Wild boars will not separate me from my dear Maya again as long as I am alive." He laughed as he added, "all this sappy talk is making me hungry. Let's go in to dinner and make plans for a happy future on full stomachs."

Kamala and Biju joined them for dinner before they all retired to their rooms for the night.

Chapter Twenty Three

When flights of fancy carry me away on a cloud
a touch, a kiss, and
you bring me back to my heaven on earth
        Shakuntala Rajagopal

The next morning they drove back to Trivandrum, and together they went to see Ammini Ammavi. She, Ammini Ammavi had almost fainted when they called the night before.

In anticipation of their visit, Ammini Ammavi went to the Ganesha temple early that morning and cracked seven coconuts at the steps of the temple to please Lord Ganesha. She had also done an *archana*, a special offering of flowers fruits and prayers to Lord Ganesha, especially for Radha's sake, towards an auspicious beginning of a new life. After all, that is what a mother had to do when good things happen to a daughter; and Ammini Ammavi knew only too well she was all the mother who Radha knew and remembered.

The very minute Radha alighted from the car, Ammini Ammavi was at her side. "Radha mol, here let me put the chandanam on your forehead." She placed the *chandanam*, which was the sandalwood paste that had adorned the deity of Ganesha at the temple, on Radha's forehead thus transferring Ganesha's blessings to her. She hugged Radha tight. Teary eyed, she walked over to the other side of the car, to place chandanam on Danny's forehead also. Ignoring his hand extended to greet her, she grabbed him in both arms in a bear hug! Everybody was in tears, now. Raising the loose ends of her white cotton sari she wiped away Radha's tears and reached up to wipe Danny's tears too.

"We have all shed enough tears dear children. Let us smile and plan for a future of love and happiness. When you called on the telephone last night to tell me about Danny, you made me very happy, Radha, she gushed.

She took Radha's arm in one hand, Danny's in the other and smiling happily walked them into her house for a sumptuous breakfast she forced them to eat, in spite of their protests.

Later that day Danny approached the Surgery Professor. "Dr. Raman, I have been thinking over your offer of my heading the department of Surgical Oncology at the Cancer Center. Is it still open? Or, have you already filled the spot?"

"Oh yes it is still open. I was hoping that you would decide soon and in our favor, because I cannot think of anybody more qualified to do so." Dr. Raman replied.

After a few a moment's hesitation, he continued. "There is also a very selfish interest on my part in offering you the job. I don't think I have told you about this anonymous donor that has stipulated that twenty five percent of all the work done here, patient care as well as research programs, be dedicated towards the indigent patients. This particular benefactor is willing to be an ongoing patron and will underwrite all such expenses, provided we comply with his/her request. I know that you will be the best person to look out for such an altruistic direction in the Center's services."

Danny was speechless. But only for a moment. He was awed by the timeliness of all the good fortune coming his way. He could literally have his cake and eat it too. His dreams were coming true. Not only were the challenges of the new department appealing, now he could also take care of his poor patients at a very fine center without having to justify his every movement.

His voice was hoarse and his eyes wet, as he took two steps towards the Professor's desk, shook hands with him and said. "Yes. Dr. Raman, I am very happy to accept the position and I promise you it will be one of the leading Surgical Oncology departments in this country, soon. I cannot thank you enough for this opportunity, and you will never know exactly how happy you have made me!" He shook hands with Dr. Raman, again, said the proper goodbyes and walked out. He felt as if he was walking on a cloud.

"Maya! Tell me you are proud of me! You are looking at the Chief of Surgery at the Cancer Center. I am certain that it is written in the stars that we are to be together! One year ago, I would not even have considered this position." He laughed a nervous laugh. "What you don't know is I almost refused to attend these meetings. I do believe that my love for you, no, *our love* was powerful enough to drag me over here, now. I am in seventh heaven and I don't really want to come down to Earth."

"I have always been proud of all your accomplishments. Even when I did not have the opportunity to share the moments with you, I have always glowed inwardly when I heard of the great deeds you were doing. I agree it was fate that brought us back together. Maybe my prayers had something to do with it also. Although I had no hope of ever being with you again, still, I have always prayed for your success and happiness."

"Did you for one minute think that I would be happy apart from you Maya? Even breathing was painful when I was away from you. Separated from you, I worked extra long hours until I was too exhausted to feel, and all the while I was punishing myself for having left you. For having let you go. I should have stayed and fought harder."

"We don't ever have to be separated, darling. I will never ever leave or let you leave me. But, before we can finalize the plans as to how we are going to keep these promises to ourselves we have to go see your little girl and explain to her what we intend to do."

"I agree with you, dear, let us go finish up on all the meetings and get out of here. I already called and spoke to my Amma about us. She is going to tell Sheenu that I will be coming over soon, and that I wanted her to come and live with me from now on. I am sure Amma will tell her about us, at least as much as she can understand."

As soon as their meetings and commitments with the opening ceremonies were over they drove up to Cochin to Danny's Amma's house. On their way, he filled in Radha all the details of Sheenu's young life.

"I tried to cope with raising a child without the mother's presence." Danny felt he had to explain his actions to Radha. "Every time Sheenu was ill or needed any special attention, I felt inadequate and helpless. Although I could afford the best nannies in town, when for various reasons one of them left and there was a turnover, I saw the pain and the confusion in the little girl's eyes. Also, when Sheenu was old enough to ask questions about her mother's absence, I felt angry that for no fault of her own, the young child was deprived of her mother's love. I was taking out my frustrations on her, and that was not fair, either."

Danny had to stop talking because the bad memories still hurt. "When we went to visit Amma, she suggested that I leave Sheenu with her. First I was morally offended that she questioned my paternal competence. But once I returned to Delhi with Sheenu, I realized she needed a more stable daily routine than a father who was on call for his patients twenty four hours a day, could offer. I took her back to Amma and she has been taken good care of, since then."

"Will your Amma resent the fact I am taking her away, now?" Radha was genuinely concerned.

"Oh no, no! In the past few years Amma has been after me to remarry and to take Sheenu with me. In her eleven years, I had only shared the first two years with Sheenu, and those had been turbulent. Amma feels sorry for Sheenu having to grow up knowing her mom had practically left her, and her father had been too busy or unprepared to take care of her. Of course my Amma has made up for it in the excellent loving She has given her. But as Sheenu has gotten older, Amma has been reminding me the girl needed a mother, and that she needed a normal home."

He stopped to regain his composure. "Finally I had to tell her about us and why I could not marry for any reason other than love, again. Of course at the time of our conversation I had had no hopes of our finding each other again! Yesterday, when I told her how we are planning a future together, Amma was in tears. She is very happy for us."

Danny showed Radha pictures of an adorable little girl. But in all of her pictures, even in the ones that showed Sheenu smiling, her large dark eyes held an expression of longing and even a touch of loneliness, and Radha's heart went out to her. She promised Danny that she would adopt and raise her as her own. Danny assured her that he had no doubts whatever, about that.

When they arrived at Danny's mother's home, Sheenu was still at school.

Danny introduced Radha to his mom. "Amma, this is the light of my life and I want you to accept her as your daughter."

"Dear girl," his mom said through tears of joy, "Danny has told me all about you and all of what happened in the past. I am really happy for the two of you for having found each other again. Take it from one who has seen the world, do not toss away your opportunity for happiness. Grab it with both hands and be happy together."

She smiled and turned to Danny. "You never told me how beautiful this young lady is!" Returning her eyes to Radha she continued. "I hear I have you to thank for bringing my son closer to home in my old age. You can't imagine how much that means to me. Thank you!"

They sat down to tea and biscuits and a proud *Ammoomma*, grandmother, went on to brag about how good a student Sheenu was. She was excited that she had taken up dancing. She was a very diligent student and a hard worker.

"But," she continued with a worried look, "she does not speak much. Ever since her mother cancelled out on a vacation with her, two summers ago, she refuses to write to her mother and will not speak about her to anybody. I have tried my level best to get her to talk about it. I know she is hurting, but she will not let me help her."

Radha's eyes got misty just thinking of the eleven year old, who was obviously lonely for her mother. She prayed that she could make a good mother to her. She vowed to herself never to let her devotion to Danny or her patients come between this young girl who she was going to acquire as a daughter.

Radha remembered how Ammini Ammavi had taken care of her, when her own mother died. She could not imagine what would have happened to her without Ammini Ammavi as her surrogate mother.

Suddenly the door opened and Sheenu walked in, placed her school books on the table and hastily ran to her father. He hugged her close and kissed her.

"Daddy, daddy, you're home! I could not concentrate on anything the teacher said in class, all day!" She spoke in a soft melodious voice. Then she shyly looked up towards Radha, unsure of what was expected of her.

"Yes Sheenu-mol," he replied, "I am home. How would you like to come home with me after this school session? Come and meet Dr. Radha. I'm sure Ammoomma has told you all about her."

Sheenu got away from her father's arms.

"So this is Dr. Radha?" She moved slowly towards Radha. "Did my Ammoomma tell you I don't have a Mother?" The pleading in her voice brought tears to Radha's eyes.

Radha stepped forward and taking both of the little girl's hands in hers she knelt down beside her. In the softest of voices she spoke to Sheenu looking directly into her sad eyes.

"Your Ammoomma told me what a good student you are, and would you believe me if I tell you that I've always wanted a daughter? Would you come and live with me and your Daddy and be my special daughter, also?"

The little girl looked up uncertainly at her Ammoomma, and saw that her Ammoomma was in tears. Ammoomma nodded acquiescence to her.

Sheenu took the hint and moving into Radha's arms muttered "I never thought I'd get a mother again. I want a mother, and if you will be my mother, I promise to be a very good girl." She too was crying.

Danny knelt on the floor by them and crying unashamedly, gathered the newly found mother-daughter duo to his bosom in a tight embrace.

His voice was a bare whisper. "I love you both dearly, and will never ever let anything separate us. I thank you Maya, from the bottom of my heart for reuniting me with my daughter."

Seated happily between an adoring father and her new mother, basking in their love and attention, Sheenu filled their ears and hearts with incessant chatter about her dancing lessons, her friends and her teachers. All the way back home to Trivandrum she held on tight to Radha's hand as if she was afraid that she would lose her if she let go.

In Trivandrum they took Sheenu to Kamala's house to make friends with Kamala's daughter Bindu. In no time the two young girls were busy talking about dolls and games and books that they were reading.

Now, it was Radha's turn to visit her favorite Krishna Temple to pray and offer thanks. Danny accompanied her and stood silently savoring the beautiful sight of her radiant face engulfed in a glow of devotion and watched the peace in her eyes, proud that he had finally given her the joy she rightfully deserved.

When they left the temple, he drove to the garden behind their old Medical college. The jasmines were in bloom and the Cypress trees waved them a warm welcome as they alighted at their own special corner of the world.

He opened the blessed offerings from the temple and chose some red kumkum powder and with his right ring finger placed a perfectly round bindu *(thilakam)* on the center of her forehead. Radha was weeping with joy. Then gently he lifted her teary yet radiant face up to his and muttered softly. "My placing this *thilakam* on your forehead hereby releases you from your widowhood, Maya. Even if I die before you do, you are never to erase it from your forehead. The marriage of our hearts is immortal and the physical parting will not affect our union. You have to promise me that."

"I do so promise, Danny." Her voice was barely audible as she melted into his arms.

Printed in the United States
105783LV00002B/16-111/A